MOTHER IS A COUNTRY

Kathrin Perutz

MOTHER
IS A COUNTRY

A POPULAR FANTASY

HARCOURT, BRACE & WORLD, INC., NEW YORK

For the MacDowell Colony
with all my thanks

MOTHER IS A COUNTRY

"He's killed himself again. The bastard."

"Dead, is he?"

"That'll be the day. Here, gimme a hand."

Between them they roped John Scudley like a hammock, swinging his inert mass from side to side as they carried him to the ambulance. Repugnance showed on the meaty faces of the bearers; they turned thick noses up and away from this sissy, this un-American blob of unconscious humanity, and when the first turned to grip the ankles from the front to more easily steer the mock corpse into the white hold, he leered. "What a wet blanket. Let's fold him up army-style."

"Like the American flag," said his partner, though when they actually deposited him on the cot inside, their movements remembered gentleness.

The small crowd was disappointed. Cargo laded, the ambulance shivered to life; the men leaped on, the siren began to wail. No escort, not even a police car. No blood, no weeping relatives, not one hysterical woman. "John Scudley again," the grocer explained to the butcher, who shrugged his shoulders and moved off. Scudley's landlord, always a literalist, was rubbing his hands on his jeans as though to wash them of the whole business. People dispersed, backs weary with another spectacle that hadn't come off, their shoulders resigned to failure, as though the projector had broken down before the end of a movie where they had gotten in free and so had no way of demanding

3

their money back. A few of the more hardy or more phlegmatic lingered in hopes of a sequel but then they, too, wandered off and lunch hour was over, having provided no main course, nothing to feed the scavengers.

At the hospital, Scudley's stomach was lustily pumped and within a few hours the patient regained whatever consciousness he may have possessed when he tried to lose it. His first desire was for water; then for the priest. When the latter arrived, Scudley looked at him with small, bloated, disappointed eyes. "You're not the one who used to be here."

"No," answered the priest, "I'm Father Niemans."

"What kind of name is that?"

"My own. My Christian name."

"Any saints by that name?" Scudley asked suspiciously, feeling his stomach seek entrance to his throat.

"Not that I know of." The priest, Scudley decided, was impertinent. First of all, he was too young. Second, too tall; third, too good-looking: a movie actor playing the part of priest who in the end renounces the cloth for Debbie Reynolds or Doris Day.

"What order?"

"Franciscan."

"Impossible," decreed Scudley and fell asleep.

When he woke, the priest was still there. He tried to shoo him away with his hand, then by turning over, closing his eyes and emphatically pushing out his buttocks. "I hear," said Father Niemans, "You're not Catholic."

"Of course not," mumbled Scudley, pulling the blankets over his head.

"Then why did you ask for me?"

It was warm, dark and delicious. "Go away now, Father." A few slight movements and Scudley was settled perfectly in his nest. "I'm getting ready to dream now and that's blasphemy, you old . . ."

This time the man left. Scudley turned on his back,

4

yawned, and began to evaluate the situation. Another failure. This was—he calculated—his seventh attempt in the past five years, the first of these on his thirtieth birthday. Earlier attempts didn't count; they had been committed in total blindness of soul, in youth; careless acts like discarding an old newspaper from a moving car, only to have it fly back and cover up the windshield. He thought of pigeons in a row and aimed his forefinger at them, shooting them down with a little ping! in the forehead of each. Seven dead pigeons, scrawny legs sticking up from plump bellies, hairy tooth-picks stuck in meaty cushions. Or maybe they were sea gulls. Anyway, there they were, a straight line of them on the beach. Crabs crawled up to nuzzle them, moved backwards, each with his piece of flesh; and though the meat was white, the crabs turned red eating it, until the ocean was the color of blood.

Seven times in five years. Enough to make you puke. And even this time, the conventional way, the old reliable barbi-turate that controlled population in the privileged classes, even with safe and sure Seconal, it hadn't worked. The other failures could be put down to extravagance, overindulgence, theatricality. But this time he had done it the way everyone did, a slew of red-bellied monsters, hoarded in spite of the new food-and-drug act, gathered for over five months in a little silver box. How sad, he thought: all those sleek tiny bombs in the damn hospital pump. Not one of them left. He'd taken such care to collect them, keep them cool. He'd given such attention to them, examining them every day to make sure their skins weren't melting or cracked or pustular. Just goes to show. You try to conform, try to do things the usual way and squoosh! out it goes, just like the rest of it. Every-thing comes out in the end. Proves there's no point being a conformist. Russian roulette next time. Worked with that poet. Unusual, newsworthy. But chances are six to one against. Risky, that. Still, worth giving a whirl.

* * *

5

Mike MacGrogan, Scudley's boss, was furious. "Not again. No. It's too much. And how long," he inquired of a subordinate, "does this punk expect me to put up with his shenanigans? I won't take it. No more. And to think," he added incredulously, the new thought breaking on him like rain over a desert, "to think it's always on company time! Never on a weekend, no. Scudley's too smart for that. Sly little weasel. I'll fox him. He can't come back here, no, for no reason whatsoever, none. This is the end!" He glowered at the man and strutted out, briskly, past the rows of breakfast cereals and detergents.

Here it was, among the cans and boxes, red-white-and-blue cylinders, sani-sealed bologna, pink and yellow bottles, vacuum-packed sponges and brushes, bags of chocolate kisses, dog food, baby food, steak untouched by human hands, life-size mama dolls and baby dolls, garlic and garlic presses, fresh dill, iceberg lettuce, diet peaches, pâté from Strasbourg, Band-Aids, ribbons, lace doilies, flowered toilet paper, spices, herbs, kosher bacon, yoghurt, Liederkranz and Swiss jams, here in the emporium of taste and tastelessness, where paper, metal, glass or plastic were all that fingers could know of texture, where all smells fused in one hard, clean, disinfectant odor, here Scudley had spent years daydreaming of something cleaner, smoother, more sensually neutral, non-returnable and hermetically sealed than anything around him. He daydreamed, while pushing the cart down the aisles, arranging stacks, retrieving fallen cans, stuffing large paper bags, assisting housewives, doing inventory, drinking beer, washing floors, adjusting the air conditioner or loud-speaker, of an act only he could perform: a unique, one-way act without stamps, coupons or receipts, an act that would show the bastards and zombies there was life in him yet.

Sometimes he drew inspiration from the shelves: a grinning tiger on the cornflakes box suggested the thought of locking himself in the zoo at night, in a cage with mother

6

tigers, there to have limbs torn from his body and be eaten by voracious felines. The submarine gun on another cereal box had Scudley musing—for hours—on the possiblity of shooting himself under water, until rationality argued that to procure such a gun, a boat to take him to the middle of the ocean and weights to hold him down (he instinctively floated up whenever submerged) was a venture with little chance of success in a town so far away from the sea. While his fellow employees listened to the tops in pops or studied nudie magazines, Scudley dreamed of death. And though he felt no contempt for the frivolity of other men's lives, he found no one in whom he could confide, no one with whom to share the pink-and-yellow (sometimes effervescent) dreams of killing himself. He knew he would be thought antisocial and so, like a lonely pervert, Scudley hugged his secret to himself and it became sweeter, more precious the longer he guarded it. But no one knew how exquisite was the fantasy and when word came that Scudley had done it again, Mac-Grogan's opinion of the matter was the one generally accepted at the supermarket.

At the university, however, a dissenting opinion was held, at least by Marya Poum, the only professor who had ever heard of John Scudley and the sole member of the academic body to have been in his bed. Dr. Poum was in her early thirties; her eyes were very dark and her bosom almost fabled in possessing those proportions reserved for earthy heroines in novels by male authors. A professor of English, Dr. Poum was aware of her literary dimensions and accepted the admiration of her students as reverence due her natural ability to make literature as erotic and comforting as a mother. The hospital phoned during office hours; her free hand rushed to her heart, then sidled up until it could firmly grasp her throat, where fingertips explored the firmness of tendons. Her thighs trembled, moved apart and

7

when she replaced the receiver she closed her eyes so that the student sitting opposite would disappear.

"Something wrong, Dr. Poum?" asked the young man with an older man's solicitude.

"Emergency. Hospital. Friend—suicide attempt." Marya Poum, honored and titled for her intimacy with the English language, allowed herself the luxury of abandoning it whenever she felt the situation crucial enough. Speechlessness in moments of intensity was, she knew, an indication that her emotions had been deeply stirred and that even her fine, scholarly mind—the male in her—could capitulate in the flood of surging reality.

"How terrible," said the young man. "Can I get you anything? You don't look well. Water?"

"Brandy."

Impotent to fulfill her request, the young man removed the burning cigarette from between his lips and handed it to her. She sucked deep and gratefully. "You come," she breathed, "some other time. I must go now."

"Yes, professor. I hope he's all right, your friend."

She looked at him sharply, suspecting malice in the use of her title and the suspicion restored her sense of control. "Thank you, Mr. Willis. I'll see you again on Thursday at three-fifteen. Good afternoon." She rose, the majestic and— now again—formidable length of her, fidgeted the papers on her desk into a neat pile, snuffed out the cigarette and marched out to her car. "Poor Scudley," she said aloud, caressing the knob of the gearshift. "Poor baby."

The victim—or object—of her consternation was fast asleep and Dr. Poum was asked to return later. To the professor, this request was a mark of insolence, and to the she-goat of a redheaded receptionist, she explained in a voice where control thinly sheathed tumescent exasperation: "I have no patience with formalities. I have not come here in order to be seen by the patient but in order to see him.

Therefore, it makes no difference whether he is conscious or not. I should like to speak to someone more competent than you."

The receptionist glowered and either swallowed her gum or spat inwardly. "Those are my orders. You'll have to leave."

Further colloquy was useless, Marya realized, but at the door she turned and advanced upon the desk with new determination. "I'm *Dr.* Poum and if you further attempt to impede my visit to Mr. Scudley, I shall insure that you are dismissed peremptorily."

"Doctor?" She cocked her head to one side and the left earring drooped to rest on her jugular vein.

"Doctor."

"Well, I don't think . . ."

"That is obvious, young lady. Which room?"

Congratulating herself on firmness of purpose and duplicity, Marya Poum entered the sickroom. The patient looked unfamiliar and she squinted down at him, rearranging his face in her mind. She remembered then that she had met him only twice before, the first time buying eggs and the second going home with him after he'd loaded the groceries into her car. Nevertheless, she looked down at him now with maternal anxiety and her lips formed a kiss for all unfortunate men who had drowned or killed themselves, fallen in war or off mountains. Imperiously, she imposed her benediction on the room and on all its inhabitants of past and future. Her body held erect by mercy, she marched out almost into the arms of the handsome young priest, who, before entering possible cinematic purgatory with a button-nose star, was continuing his rounds of comfort.

"Oh," said the priest, stepping back to avoid contact with Marya's nipples.

"Forgive me, Father," she whispered in a tone suggesting passionate contrition for a multitude of sins.

"You're a friend of Mr. Scudley?"

9

"Ah." Her eyes grew sad and browner. "Marya Poum. Dr. Marya Poum."

"Father Niemans. Forgive me for asking you questions at a time like this. I realize you must be extremely upset. . . ."

"Ah, Father." Her lashes sank gently and she had visions of all the powerful men represented by the young priest: bishops, cardinals, saints, the Pope even. . . . She shuddered.

"But I wondered if you could tell me why Mr. Scudley asked for me, since he's not Catholic."

So often in her daydreams she lay dying, usually after rape and a stab in the belly. In the white room, her mauve nightdress translucent and frilly, her skin dewed with moisture, she whispered her request for a priest. He looked like the one here, his eyes were green (later to redden and flood with tears) and he listened to her confession for hours, made the sign of the cross over her, kissed her lips, eyes, shoulders, bosom and then, holding her hand, guided her gently (she in mauve, he in black, the cloak opening wider and wider as they ascended) to shades beyond, where white birds fluttered their paper wings and cooed along the vertebrae. Everything must be done with elegance and ritual. Tragic love, awakened in this hour of death, brought absolution which only literature could offer. "I understand him," she said. "One needs to feel the prick of destiny."

"But he's just committed a mortal sin. I can't baptize him into the Faith."

"No need, Father. Just bring him to the light. Guide him as Virgil did Dante."

Father Niemans frowned and his eyes inadvertently fell on the literate, heaving protrusion of Marya's body. "I'm not qualified to do that," he said. "But I could say a few 'Our Fathers.'"

"Yes"—she smiled sweetly—"do that. The poor man. Here's my card. When he wakes up, tell him I was here. I'll

10

come again tomorrow after Pope to Johnson." His eyes moved over her naked arms, then back to her face. The thought that he could be a virgin disturbed her deliciously.

When Scudley woke up, he scratched. "Measly, mousy masturbator," he said to no one in particular. He was conscious, damn it, and the room was flooded with roses, cinnamon, orchids. Smells of the deceased. If one could get astride oneself and wring one's neck—Scudley smiled at himself; he was being silly. Frozen raspberries in mock turtle soup, Wheaties in the dishwasher, green stamps fluttering, snowing down, turning plaid, caught in the drift . . . a giant pickle and on its nose, dried milk. Steaks oozing their blood down rivers of chocolate syrup; a white blanket of paper napkins—nice, that—now lacy, doilies of the deathbed. Plump starlets wrapped in tissue paper, one veil, next, more, pink, yellow, blue-rose, but the last won't come off, stuck on with honey. He wiped himself with one and threw her in the freezer. She turned into a mango, at the center an egg. You open it: blanched almonds and sardines. Swimming through yoghurt—an island, no, fresh-frozen blueberry pie with baby onions. He threw up, and again, dry vomit, paper coupons, box tops, silver cigarette paper, labels coming undone. . . . A nurse looked in and saw him shaking in the bed. "Are you all right?"

"Peanuts," he spat at her. "Shit."

"There, there, you'll be all right now, honeybun," she called stickily.

"Bitch," he said, but she was gone. "Bloody bitch with ketchup, chili sauce, Tabasco, mustard, relish, marshmallow whipped-cream soy sauce. Wrapped in Saran, special process comes out like new. Secret ingredient builds you up eight different ways the new vitality food shake vigorously. Keep cool after opening pry up with knife. No more messy

11

hands." He retched again: cornflakes rubbing against Rice
Krispies. Maybe he could vomit himself into eternity.

> . . . till e-ter-na-ty, oh
> won't you please be
> be my little baby
> be my
> be my little baby
> be my baby now-ow,
> woe woe woe woe woe

A spasm of well-being. Through the half-open door he
watched nurses, doctors, beds, orderlies, visitors go by.
Father Niemans passed, leading with his pelvis as do all
American men brought up with the concept of a horse between their legs. Scudley smiled. God is the backward dog
with his master's voice; three for a buck. Nine out of ten
doctors prefer St. Joseph. Good for your child. He felt
light and contented. Everything pumped from his stomach,
all the crap sucked out, a hollow cylinder with four limbs,
like a woman after abortion. Cleaned out; nobody could
suspect the former misconception.

When Father Niemans strutted back again he stopped to
inform Scudley, "Dr. Poum was here to visit you."

"Doctor what?"

"Poum."

"Don't know any Poum," he pouted.

"Young woman, teaches at the university, I think."

"Mare!"

"What?"

"Mare. Her name's Marya, I call her Mare. Met her
among the eggs. Large, brown, grade A."

"I see. You were sleeping. She said to tell you she'd be
back tomorrow."

Scudley beamed at the priest. It was very nice of Mare to
come galloping over, he thought. She'd been so coltish when
he'd asked to see her again. But she was a good egg, that

12

Mare. Venus, all-new-redi-set oysters on the half-shell. A pearl of a dish. Enjoy it summer or winter, just look for the sign of Venus, the mound of oysters where Venus . . .

". . . venial sin can therefore be forgiven. But mortal sin cannot," Father Niemans was explaining. "Though contrition is always possible. Even imperfect contrition is enough for the forgiveness of mortal sin if absolution in confession is added. For venial sin, imperfect contrition alone suffices."

"I see," he said, closing his eyes. "But I'm tired now."

The priest turned to leave. "God bless you."

Less work for Mother, thought Scudley.

In madras Bermudas, knobby knees protruding above hairy, bowlegged calves, the Joint Chiefs of Staff guided her through the restaurant. Around their necks, the red handkerchiefs gave them a raffish, unkempt look and bright roses bursting on the short-sleeved shirts made waiters turn their eyes from the awesome presence. Red-and-white-checkered tablecloths sprouted on all sides and, when the colorful posteriors of the Joint Chiefs of Staff swished by them, the brightness was almost too much for Marya to bear. But she was very happy. The Secret Service man kept his distance and the proprietor was oily. The Joint Chiefs of Staff were distracted; romance was not their racket and the tables, candlelight, violins schmaltzing through the smell of oregano didn't inspire them as Marya had hoped. She opened her pocketbook and pulled out a penis. "Here is your pecker, sirs."

"Thanks, ma'am," they said and strapped it on. "Never trust ourselves without one. You gotta be firm these days."

The proprietor oozed up rubbing his hands. The Joint Chiefs of Staff ordered veal scaloppini for them and a Chianti which Marya judged too sweet and heavy. "I don't want to interfere," she murmured with feminine languor, "but couldn't we have a Vieto?"

"Give the lady what she wants," they commanded.

Afterwards, down long halls, down perspiring corridors, the Secret Service man yelping and prancing behind, Marya and the Joint Chiefs of Staff walked to their room. The

Secret Service man did a little dance with arms fluttering, lashes batting and feet skipping to the music of a gypsy snake charmer. His voice, a small reed instrument, was piping and breathless. "Bring our G.I.'s home," he chanted, and sighed. "Oh please, Staff baby, bring our boys back home."

"He's disrespectful," opined Marya and all of them entered the room. The Joint Chiefs of Staff unzipped their flies with care, as though a Top Secret rested underneath; the Secret Service man let his trousers fall around his feet, was incapable of walking and could only pitch forwards and back. Marya, naked and glistening, her hair crackling like birch twigs, spread her thighs. The men coupled one with another, a congo line of leapfrogs wagging their tails. Marya whinnied a little, remembering that tomorrow was Election Day and she, elector and elected, was now holding the hot line. She felt proud to be so involved. She understood the meaning of secret service. "I need some, too," she said and the Joint Chiefs of Staff gallantly turned her over.

"Hell," she said, waking up abruptly, "what a time to stop." In the afternoon, after Pope-Johnson, she could continue. But it wouldn't be as good, she thought sadly, because of all the manipulation that would have to go into it. This was the third night she had spent with the Joint Chiefs of Staff and she had learned to put up with their quirks. Kinky, they are, she thought, though she found them extremely attractive. Power roared out from them like a volcano of aphrodisiacs. They represented the fall of angels; they were sexy as hell. Like mastiffs, mass stiffs, powerful enough to screw everybody. She would be their Boswell, boss well. She smiled and stroked herself. "You'll die, sir, either on the gallows or of the pox." "That depends, my Lord, whether I embrace your politics or your mistress." Where was that said? Medmenham Abbey? Beefsteak Club? She'd have to look it up; the clubs of Georgian England were a necessary adjunct to the study of Augustan literature.[1]

[1] Her second guess was correct. This interchange, between the Earl of

15

At breakfast, she chewed off too large a piece of English muffin and choked. Tears streaming down her face, she reassured herself: *"Noli me tangere*, for Caesar's I am,/And wild for to roam, though I seem tame."* [1] Anne Boleyn. Belonged first to Wyatt, then the King. Embracing the mistress first, the politics later and dying comfortably of old age. Henry was too risky. A penny for your head. Drunk for a penny, dead drunk for tuppence.[2] Her throat was cleared and, eyes red, blinking, she peered into the day.

"Where's Mare?" he asked petulantly.

"Mère?" Poor boy. Thirty-five years old and homesick.

"Yeah. Where is she? Didn't you say she was coming this afternoon?"

"Oh. Your friend."

"And she's not here. She's forgotten about me."

Indeed, Marya had forgotten. Only the nonexistence of Scudley interested her; now that he existed, the thought of him was tedious, like garbage that must be emptied, and she put it out of her mind. When a priest phoned, identifying himself as Father Niebuhr or Nietzsche, she said, "Cuddly? Cuddly? I don't know any Cuddly."

Sandwich and John Wilkes, took place at the Beefsteak Club, which was dedicated to two ideals: noble steak and sparkling wit. The quotation has become apocryphal and may be found in several variations. For one, see: Jones, Louis C., *The Clubs of the Georgian Rakes*. Columbia University Press. New York, 1942. P. 144. Wilkes' reply in this version is: "That depends upon this—whether I embrace your Lordship's principles or your mistress."

[1] From the poem "Who So List to Hunt" by Sir Thomas Wyatt (1503–1542), spelling modernized. "Caesar" refers to King Henry VIII.

[2] A common eighteenth-century English advertisement until the Tippling Act of 1751, which abolished distillers' licenses and prohibited illegal distilling. Consumption of gin had, by that time, increased twenty times (2000 per cent) since the Revolution of 1688 and England boasted one alehouse to each eighty inhabitants. See: Turberville, A. S., *English Men and Manners in the Eighteenth Century*. Galaxy Books, Oxford University Press. New York, 1960. P. 228; and Williams, E. N., *Life in Georgian England*. B. T. Batsford Ltd. London, 1963. P. 112.

"No, Scudley. John Scudley."

"Oh yes. He works in the supermarket. Is he alive?"

"Very much so. And he would be greatly pleased if you were to visit him."

"But . . ." Something was on the agenda for this afternoon, though she couldn't remember what. Her left hand reached for her appointment book but the only entries for today were: "Tide Dove Twinkle (2) Call V. Shoe repair" and lower down, an afterthought: "TLS Life (p. 34)." "Not today." She remembered: a session with the Joint Chiefs behind closed doors.

"Tomorrow then? He's very anxious to see you."

"Father Kneeband . . ."

"Mans."

"Kneeman, I wish you'd explain to him. I don't really know him well at all. I'm very busy now, it's near the end of the semester, you see, I don't want to seem unkind but I really haven't the time to visit chance acquaintances in the hospital."

"Very well." His voice was curt; she liked the growl of his bilabial fricative.

"Perhaps . . ."

"Yes?"

"Are you always with him?"

"I make my rounds every afternoon."

"At this time?"

"Approximately."

"I'll be there tomorrow." A man of God also represented the power structure of the Church. Nearer my God to thee. Under cover of a habit, things could sprout and come forth. The Medmenham Monks had used the motto of Thélème: *Fay ce que Vouldras.*[1]

"Fine. I'll give Mr. Scudley your message. Good afternoon."

"Yes."

[1] See footnote on p. 87.

17

She rocked the receiver in its cradle a moment before letting go. She locked the door to her office, pulled the blinds and went to lie down on the couch. No need to remove anything. Strutting down the halls—she clad them properly this time, in business suits and Hermès ties—they were flanked by the Secret Service man. Into a gilded suite, lights dim but enough to make out forms, aroma of balsam, very warm—you're an unpresidented pervert, she told herself—one entering from the front, five at the rear and the Secret Service man spurring them on. Two young ladies at hand for the breasts, spectators coming. A howl from the head of state, jabs, the body politic firm and incisive, words erupting with dental and velar stops, explosion, susurration and glide. The liaison is not made with *les haricots* . . . she dozed.

"Damn beans," said Mike MacGrogan, "I knew we shouldn't have ordered them. Who needs French beans anyway? People here don't eat like frogs. I could've told you that. Damn frogs and their froggy stringbeans. I'd like to shoot it right back at them, shoot it up their . . ."

A lady customer walked by and smiled sweetly. MacGrogan gave a quick nod. "I heard about the dreadful thing," she said. "It's dreadful."

"Who told you? No one's supposed to know what we order. Just a little mistake; it'll all be straightened out. Buy American, that's my motto. You can't go wrong. And I'm right, our beans beat theirs any day. American housewives know it, too; they just won't cotton to this foreign stuff."

She looked at him with amazement. "Beans? Where do beans come in?"

She remained unenlightened while Mike MacGrogan was called to the phone. Tsk-tsking quietly, she wheeled her cart past baby and pet foods to the Diet Section for noncaloric chocolate fudge. On her way out, she again ran into the manager. "I don't know what you meant about the beans. I was talking about poor John Scudley, poor man."

"I've had as much as I can take from him. More. That last time was once too many."

"You mean he's not coming back?"

"Exactly what I had in mind, ma'am."

"But Mr. MacGrogan, surely you won't deprive the poor deluded man of his job. Why, that's probably the only thing he has to live for." Realizing her mistake, she blushed. Mike MacGrogan waved her out airily and, passing the cashier, hissed: "No. And that's final. Stringbeans and sleeping pills. What a mess."

Neither he nor the dieting lady knew how near she had come to the truth with her accidental remark. For, if his job at the supermarket was not Scudley's precise reason for living, it was nevertheless the only way he knew how to live and his fantasies of death were a way of penetrating that life. The supermarket was Scudley's element and he loved it. Unthinkable that he should spend his days anywhere else or with a different occupation. He loved the colors, shapes and cool textures of things; he loved the variety within monotony; he found pleasure in being constantly among people, observing and helping them, exchanging a word or two while not being called upon to give evidences of friendship or any greater effort of sympathy than was needed to assist in the search for a special brand of tuna fish. Among objects, Scudley was free. In this atmosphere of buying, choosing, complaining, loading; in this bright temple of riches that fed America and kept her strong, in this great provider of the Great Society, a man could become as altruistic, ignored and carefully labeled as anything on the shelves. If not the acme of contentment, here was at least a foothill. The problems of fellow Americans amused Scudley, though he didn't really understand them. Peace was so easy to attain. He never had to worry what he should wear to work; if he forgot to shave one morning, there were no reproaches. He had enough money to buy what he wanted, he received free beer and food as remuneration, he was warm in winter, cool in summer, always shrouded by soft music and, except for very occasional encounters with MacGrogan, did not have to contend with the moods and feelings of other people.

Once in a while he compared himself with other men and then pitied the poor guy in an office who had to go out with the boys, put on a cheery front, sell products through a combination of high pressure and charm, either take three hours for lunch with a client, becoming sleepy and drunk, or else take no time for lunch at all. Bad for heart, liver and digestion. Scudley had an hour for lunch every day and his products sold themselves. He wanted nothing from anyone and treated the humans in the store just as he did the objects, with genial indifference. He was home every evening at twenty minutes to six, made himself a drink, prepared dinner, watched television, took in a movie or entertained a lady he had met at work. He enjoyed cooking, was good at it (as all the ladies attested) and, though his energy as lover was erratic, he had not once since the age of eighteen proved unequal to the task. Not all his women had come from the supermarket, of course, but he had friendly green eyes, even features, broad shoulders and the housewives' demand for him was often more than what he could supply. They wanted to consume him conspicuously but he held them off. Scudley never understood the fame of Hollywood or Washington scandals; from what he knew of suburban wives, they got away with twice as much as any actress and were smarter about it, too. And those foreigners? Give him a typical American housewife any time, who could bake her cake, then a second, and have one with her lover, the other with her husband and children.

Scudley was as obvious, uncomplicated and potentially rewarding as a frozen chocolate cake. All the ingredients were

20

there, though his life had so processed them that they could not be distinguished. He felt no need for privacy because he never expected to be surprised by himself and, unlike those who have that need, did not feel within him the existence of survivors who would have to be rescued by a careful search party. There was, however, a secret side to Scudley, not distinct or separate but always present, functional and, like a female contraceptive, often not felt. Though he had tried love in all varieties except the family size, the secret, most precious part of Scudley was death. He loved its economy and cleanliness. Like a food pill to be taken at the onset of life, supplanting all meals, death had an efficiency and absoluteness which nothing else could rival. Alive, you had stomach troubles and cavities. You had phone calls to make, errands to run, people asking for your opinion, your taxes, advice, vote, comfort and before you knew it you were in the same rat race as everyone else. But there was a catch: though everyone was in the rat race, it was different for each and you had to do the running by yourself. You became complicated, twisted ("interesting" was another word for it) and everything had so many meanings that nothing made sense any more. A can of peaches or a tube of tooth paste had no such worries and neither did a corpse. You got packaged in silk and wood, hammered in and from then on everything took care of itself.

But, though Scudley would never have admitted it, his dreams of nonexistence had another side to them. Never in his life had Scudley committed what could be called a significant act. The dream of success was part of the American air he had always breathed. To be a man, you had to be a success and to be a success you had to do something that people would notice. Suicide would get you in the papers, and though you might have lost a life, it was fair exchange for gaining a name.

He was, in fact, not dissimilar to other men and wanted

21

what they want: a job and a woman. Now, lying in his hospital bed, attended by indifferent nurses, visited now and then by a priest who cared only for his soul, poor Scudley had no way of knowing that those two simple aspirations were out of his reach. He slept and dreamed of being put into boxes. Neither job nor woman was waiting for him; and he, like other men, would become afraid of fantasy.

3

At thirty-two, only four years after receiving her Ph.D., Marya Poum was full professor in a generally respected university. She had achieved this position not through her obvious attributes (in academia, as anywhere else, she came to realize, sleeping with important people served only to feed their appetite for self-respect: they were proud to give evidence that their impartiality was in no way influenced by physical intimacy), but through a combination of intelligence, natural talent for teaching and an excellent history of publications. She was eager to take on any course, particularly if she didn't know very much about the subject, and her general vivacity, her enthusiasm for what she taught and her ability to give the illusion that literature was connected with life made her extremely popular with students. Also, her dresses were just a bit too tight and she felt no qualms about wearing false eyelashes to class. She enjoyed university life as a diversion. Because her position was secure, she couldn't understand the struggles within the academic hierarchy. In the way that someone with a high income will insist money is unimportant, Marya enjoyed saying that academic titles were mere formalities. She had no particular ambition to rise higher in the academic world.

She was, however, extremely fond of power—a fact which amused her and to which she had once given serious attention. In fact, she had given serious attention to most everything until the age of thirty. Then, deciding that only profundity was superficial, she accepted the game, learned its

23

rules and became adept at cheating. Her adoration for power had begun mildly, in dreams. She, who was half Jewish (her mother's side), decided that Jew and fascist were battling it out in her unconscious. Then, seeing it was her mother's side that ached for boots and brutality while her father's side remained patient and rational, she ignored the analysis and enjoyed the sport for its own sake. She slept with Hitler, McCarthy, Khrushchev, Malcolm X, F.D.R., Churchill and Queen Victoria; every now and then a more appetizing but less powerful man would be admitted to her dreams and with Marlon Brando or James Bond she spent moments of minor grace. Being Head of the Department didn't tempt her; neither did Guggenheims or Fulbrights. Her only ambition, she freely admitted, was being mistress to the most powerful men in the world. She didn't care about their looks, age or politics; power transformed absolutely and, so long as she was the power behind the power, she would forgive any dictator his ugliness. She felt kinship with Catherine the Great: the Saxon princess married the acned, impotent Czar with the same magnanimity (through which she eventually had him killed)[1] that Marya felt for Joe or Adolf. You could afford charity towards a man who ruled part of the world; all power geniuses were cripples, and that's where you came in.

Marya's actual lovers, however, had all been relatively inconspicuous. Though some had achieved notoriety among certain circles, none had been a name for history and none extremely wealthy. At nineteen she had been ashamed of what was now her specialty: men with no money, no reputation, no strength and, often, no face—puppet men she manipulated for her own pleasure, a brief entertainment in which ephemeral charm replaced passion. Policemen and very handsome young athletes were her favorites, the former for their uniforms and weapons, the latter for their narcis-

[1] Oldenbourg, Zoé, *Catherine the Great.* Pantheon Books (Random House). New York, 1965. P. 250.

sism. These allowed her freedom; their self-involvement made them something like gods, who could merely deign to take her but would never court her favors. She longed to be a courtesan but the times provided little opportunity. The closest she could come was being a whore to handsome young men, who, professionally and egotistically concerned with their own bodies, remained indifferent to her as anything else but an instrument or service to be rendered. With them she was free because an object. Sometimes, she slept with men out of charity or whim; never with her students, however (in a class structure, the master is duty-bound to respect his servants), but with men like John Scudley, whose lack of response and seeming indifference to or ignorance of sex had been a challenge. Those few hours had been charming, and if Scudley had died, she might have cherished him. But he was alive and neither handsome, powerful nor, since he was in his thirties, very young.

In class today, Marya concentrated on social life in the eighteenth century—breakfast concerts in Bath under Beau Nash, Sir Robert Walpole's wines and food, his chocolate bill (enough to keep three footmen for a year),[1] the Mohocks—young bloods who terrorized the streets assaulting women and murdering old men for the fun of it—pirates, bandits, Sir Francis Dashwood, clubs, pubs and coffee-houses.[2] The lecture was enormously appreciated, applauded at the end, and after class so many students came up to ask questions or volunteer comments ("They were pretty up-to-date, weren't they?") that she wasn't able to leave until twenty minutes to four.

At the hospital she learned that John Scudley had been released; she asked for Father Niemans and waited decorously in the visitors' lounge, alone.

[1] Plumb, J. H., *Men and Centuries*. Houghton Mifflin Co. Boston, 1963. Pp. 76–78.
[2] See footnote on Mohocks on p. 120; for Sir Francis Dashwood, see footnote on Medmenham Abbey, p. 87.

25

"Dr. Poum," he said with surprise.

"Father."

"Mr. Scudley has been released."

"They told me. I wanted to see you." She looked him straight in the eyes but in the end she, not he, was forced to look away. She noticed, where the sleeves of his robe fell back, the strong, blond hairs on his forearm. "Many things" —she sighed—"trouble me. You'll probably not believe it, but I've never known a priest. Oh, I've spoken to a few, here and there, in Italy or Spain, but only while visiting monasteries or churches. There's so much I'd like to learn."

"About Catholicism?"

"That too." She appraised him from under her false lashes. He was appraising her also, the blue eyes traveling smoothly over the length of her, coming to rest on her left shoulder. There's heaven in your eyes, she thought, nearer, my God, to thee. "Why did you become a priest?"

He smiled. "My mother asked me that once. To heal people, I suppose."

There are many ways of healing, she thought, and they point to the same end, which is incurable. "Didn't you ever think of what you'd have to give up? A family, women?"

"I had to be free to move, like St. Paul."

"Why? Isn't chastity difficult?"

"The Church has decreed there must be witnesses to the Second Coming. Though"—was it humor in his eyes or something else?—"I admit it's not immediately imminent. Still, freedom of movement is essential for a priest."

"Ah, mobility. And here we are. You're free to move up and down hospital corridors, in and out of rooms and wards. And I'm free to drive, walk, fly, ride. Each American averages nine thousand miles a year and housewives even more. We're a God-fearing country; all of America moves every three years."

"Really?"

26

"Buckminster Fuller.[1] But the way up and the way down are the same, aren't they? And the way in and the way out."

Inadvertently he looked down at his leg to see if it was being pulled. "Have you ever had instruction?"

"No. I'd like to." The path to glory. Baptized with fire.

"Perhaps we could arrange it. My monastery isn't far from here and you could come every week."

"Oh yes. But," she asked hopefully, "won't I desecrate it?"

"There's a common room."

They made the necessary arrangements. She was to start next Monday and they would see how far it went. She could learn the Creed if she wanted but not, as she had wished, in Latin. He desired her to understand; she wanted voodoo. They shook hands, and when Marya returned to her sky-blue Triumph, something was fluttering inside her, like a dove; or perhaps it was an eagle, like the one on the Great Seal, getting ready to soar.

Mike MacGrogan wasn't really a bad guy, he just hated weaklings. Third-generation Irish-American, powerfully built, with bloodshot eyes and a fleshy nose, Mike had a distaste for everything that wasn't true blue. He disliked minorities, foreigners, cripples and sickness; women he could tolerate if they were short and strong like his wife or slender and fair-haired like his daughter. But Mike MacGrogan, who— by the grace of God—had made something of himself through his own efforts and was on speaking and drinking terms with various members of the hagiography, could not tolerate anyone who was yellow-bellied or Red. War should be fought with vigor, troops, cunning and as much ammunition as possible. Men should be as brave and virile as the ancient heroes of Ireland or the pioneers. Scudley's suicide

[1] Fuller, Buckminster, *Education Automation*. Southern Illinois University Press. Carbondale, Illinois, 1962. Pp. 27–28.

attempt was unmanly, sick and un-American. MacGrogan felt no private animosity and showed no particular prejudice when he fired Scudley; a supermarket, like America itself, had to be kept safe for democracy, and if everyone started killing themselves, we'd be no better off than the Japs. Though they weren't doing too badly . . . still, being a kamikaze was different, and taking an overdose of sleeping pills was as bad as demonstrating or reading poetry. Beatniks, peaceniks and now this deathnik: all alike, a soppy mess of foreigners. (Yet he could be very gentle and always brought his wife breakfast in bed on the first day of her period, an event he commemorated by never letting his eyes rest on her face.)

The news hit Scudley with a quick jab to the kidneys. Denied entrance at the temple because he was unclean. He couldn't crawl back to where he belonged. He felt very sorry for himself. Worcestershire sauce, toilet paper, instant tea and lobster bisque were given sanctuary while he remained in the cold. He'd show that bastard. He'd do something unforgettable, perhaps even unforgivable, and the invisible eye would fling open the glass doors for the swaggering hero. But first he had to get a meal. MacGrogan had condescended to give him a week's pay and, with a bundle of bills nestling against his right buttock, Scudley went into a diner.

He ordered the special: roast beef and Yorkshire pudding. The gray thing, he supposed, was the meat and the brown glob beside it the pudding. On the White House lawn he paced in a leisurely way, crushing the grass and breaking the flowers. A sea of decapitated tulips, snapdragons, larkspur. He squashed them with his foot and a whitish liquid seeped through the petals, oozed at his ankles. A guard came running with a machine gun; he was Robert MacNamara, Lee Oswald, Dean Rusk, the President himself, Frank Sinatra. He shouted "Stop!" and took aim, but Scudley wrapped himself in an American flag, swaddled himself in it so completely that only the tips of his shoes were visible and the guard lowered his gun to salute. Scudley took out a can of lighter fuel from his pocket, poured it over himself and lit a match. In the blaze, he sang lustily:

> Oh, beautiful,
> For spacious skies,
> For amber waves of grain.
> For purple mountain majesties
> Above the fruited . . .

and he was out, exterminated, only one toenail and a star to show where he died. "Fruitcake," she said and he nodded, not because he liked fruitcake but because it came free.

The cake was stale and he was ashamed of himself. These puerile daydreams had to stop; Life was staring him in the face and he had to be man enough to stare back. He had money for this week, but what would happen when the week ended? And, more important, how would he fill his days? He wanted to be buried in something; he went to the pay phone and tried to reach Marya at the university. She wasn't there and wasn't at home either. He returned to the counter, his coffee lukewarm and bilish in front of him. He was lonely, he liked the new instant espresso that had just come in ten days ago, there was nothing to do and thinking about things gave him a headache. "Do you," he addressed the man at his right, "have fantasies?"

"Fantasies?" His neighbor was a light-skinned Negro with a fixed smile. "Oh, I see what you mean." He winked and lowered his voice. "Not here I don't. I know where you can get some though. Cheap. And let me tell you, man, nothing like them in the whole town. That's a great word for them, fantasies. Gotta remember that. Which way you turned on, man? A.C. or D.C.?"

"Either," he said hopelessly.

"Greek culture or French?"

"Don't know. America's good enough for me. . . ."

"Oh, walking the dog you mean. I got your number, man.

America first, that's the ticket. Dream American. O.K., baby, here's the place. See you nine tonight." He placed two dollar bills on the counter, swiveled around and dismounted, a minuscule man who looked as though the earth had just given way under his feet and he'd fallen through. He couldn't have been more than five feet, Scudley judged.

It was a day in May. The air, if it was the breath of God, revealed that He'd been on a bender last night. Scudley walked listlessly, a feeling of weariness in his belly as though he'd given birth too often. Signs comforted him: "Drastic sale, everything slashed"; "Books Must Go"; a car-rental agency advised: "See America—the greatest land on earth" and through the glass he saw "Flying A Shell American." At the movie house they were playing "Hands Off Mommy" in Panavision and the record store was having a sale on "Psychotic Reaction" and The Animals. A small handwritten sign in the corner offered, "A free bath to anyone who'll denounce the Beatles" and next door a pet shop advertised "Dog collars for evening wear." He walked on without noticing any more what was around him.

Then he saw the laundromat, brand new, glistening and humming; on the left, a row of washing machines; on the right, dry-cleaning machines. Apathy fell away from Scudley; he came up to the glass and stared inside. Shiny linoleum floor, detergent-dispensing machine, Coke machine, candy, cigarette and gum machines; women in curlers, small children, magazines, strollers, baby carriages, a pair of high-school lovers sitting together on a bench in front of their churning laundry, arms around each other, staring at the tempest and never shaken. A feeling of love or inspiration overtook Scudley and he went inside. He stood a moment, eyes closing, and listened to the serenade of water and steam. He asked the cashier if he could see the manager and then waited, lulled by the music, oblivious to the customers in the store. Pumping and splashing, undulations in the clean white belly; aquaria of clothes, cleaned, bleached, starched and disinfected all at once. Traces of food, ink, alcohol or love were purged away. From this belly nothing was eliminated, nothing grew; everything churned about in a whirlpool of cleanliness and emerged after labor with no vestige of dirt, no clue of past turmoil. To churn in one of those! crawl in, add bleach, press the button and whoosh! . . . Scudley's reverie was interrupted by the manager, a stout woman in a blue flowered dress, her thin mustache emphasized by a mole. Scudley asked if any job was available; she narrowed her eyes at him, grabbed hold of her hips and said no. He could see, couldn't he, that they had no need of assistants? All they needed was someone to supervise and make change and Laura did that. Her mustache bristled and her body under the dress shook off exasperation at having to deal with nincompoops. He understood but became very sad. She was waiting for him to leave but he lingered, absorbed in watching the thumping or purring bellies. "They're beautiful," he told her. "You have a fabulous establishment here."

"You think so?" she asked, suspecting his flattery; but when she saw the love in his eyes, she knew she could trust him. "I get worried sometimes. I opened this place last year, took all my savings, every cent—even had to borrow some money off my old uncle. I sit back there"—her arm swept to some indefinite horizon—"and just listen to them swishing away. It's real beautiful music. And then I get worried. You seen them new paper dresses? Yeah? Well, what if they get to be the fashion? Suppose everybody gets paper dresses—we got paper diapers already anyway— and paper socks and paper shirts and paper underwear? I tell you, I get these nightmares sometimes when I'm looking through the Montgomery Ward catalog or Sears, Roebuck and everything's made of paper. Macy's is full of paper, all them big stores."

"I wouldn't worry, ma'am. You just take a philosophical approach to the whole thing. Look: even if paper dresses come in, and paper everything else, there'll be competition. Mustn't forget that; our economy's built on competition, that's what makes it strong. So all the manufacturers will be sitting there trying to think up something new and even though the gimmick in the first place was having clothes you could throw away, they'll start making them fancier and fancier. If everybody's got paper dresses, there's got to be a way to improve on them so you'll have to buy more. Like cars. You'll see, someone'll come along with the idea of *washable* paper dresses and then they'll think of long-wearing paper dresses and maybe even eternal paper dresses. And before you know it, everyone'll be back in here again, stuffing your machines." He was amazed at his eloquence and inspiration. Perhaps being so near water did it; he'd been caught up by ideas which seemed to come from someplace outside him and formed his words.

She embraced him. "Don't know your name, but you're a brilliant man. You're a saviour, that's what you are, a man after my own heart." Her eyes were beginning to fill and she looked as though she'd just swallowed a lemon. He hastened to extricate himself. "I sure wish I had a job for you," she said ardently. "Maybe in a while you could come in as an executive adviser." Her body heaved for the next embrace. Scudley waved quickly and ran out.

It would have been nice, it would have been wonderful in there, feeding those machines and watching the stuff go round and round. It might have inspired him to all sorts of things. But then, he rationalized, that would be exhausting, to have ideas popping up all the time and not be left alone. Or else the job would be monotonous, same thing every day, all those women sitting there with nothing to do but scream at their kids. He was better off free. Free? The thought astonished him. He'd never had such freedom. No job, no obligations, no need to get up in the morning or go to bed at night. He could become like one of those bohemians or simply vanish off the earth. What a weird feeling this freedom was! Rather uncomfortable, like being in a stuffy room from which the only escape is to a large party of people you don't know. Freedom made you feel like a little child; he walked into a phone booth and tried Mare's number again.

She was home this time, but said she was just on her way out. His importunities, however, and the fact that he was newly out of the hospital after having his stomach pumped free of Seconal made her relent. He could come for a drink, she said, if he came right away and stayed for no more than twenty minutes. He ran the eight blocks to her apartment and arrived breathless.

"Shouldn't you be in bed?" she asked sternly in place of welcome.

"No. Yes. I don't know." He opened his arms to her but she stepped back, sniffing the air as though something were burning. She pushed him into a chair, placed a drink in his hand and, resigning herself to twenty minutes of inescapable tedium, put on the only badge of courage she possessed: flirtation. She ruffled his hair, smiled with a touch of licentiousness and asked how he was. He shrugged and reached for her. She sidled away, packaged herself firmly in the rocking chair, adopted a sphinxlike pose and modulated her voice. "I realize it must be hard for you to talk about it— poor thing—but how does your resurrection strike you?"

"My what?"

"Resurrection. Rising from the ashes, from the dead. Lazarus, the phoenix. You were dead and brought back to life again. How does it feel?"

"My stomach's sort of wobbly."

She stared at him with disbelief. "But you had resolved to die! You were ending it all and now you're here drinking Scotch. How does it feel?"

"Fine." He grinned. "Could I have some more ice?"

"Impossible," she said and brought him some.

"You know, Mare," he began after stirring the ice with

his middle finger and licking it, "that bastard MacGrogan fired me. My boss, you know, at the store. Don't you think that was a bastardly thing for that bastard to do?"

"Terrible." An ignoramus. She wouldn't listen any more. His skin looked jaundiced.

"So I don't know what I'll be doing now, jobwise, I mean, but I want to get even. Guys like him, they have no sensitivity. They treat us like we were things. I like your hair loose that way, suits you fine. You know, Mare? You're the only one that understands. I can pour myself out to you. I feel like telling you lots of things but sometimes the words just won't come. Know what I mean? It's like eggs wanting to be chickens but they don't know how to go about doing it." He paused a moment and his eyes stroked her breasts, belly, lower down. "You're very pretty, you know?"

Her lashes shuttled quickly, her fists unclenched and she went over to kiss his forehead. Half an hour later, naked on the bed, she kissed his thighs, gathering hairs between her teeth, and he tried to tell her what was troubling him. Her lips moved around to the small of his back, his buttocks and he sat upright, staring ahead, fighting his way toward words which always flew up when he approached and mocked him from a distance. She lay back, hands behind her head, eyes closed, and let the torrent undulate around her. This was pleasure: to be in bed with an inarticulate man who will not believe his body is a gift but tries instead to offer words, whose torment is increased because he hasn't satisfied her sexually and who sits there now, victim of battle, not knowing that his only source of interest is in his defeat. He is soft and wants to penetrate her; his words are impotent and his face shows ravage. The Romantic in her responded: ruins are better than buildings and babble often more pleasurable than wit. In this organized century, one can often crave chaos. She stroked him occasionally, like a tame lizard, and then told him it was

34

time to go, she was late for dinner as it was. "I'll wait for you here," he said.

She had once had a dream in which a six-foot lizard waited in her room. When she returned (from a horse show) he shot his blood into her veins with a syringe and then climbed on her. "You most certainly won't. I can't have anyone staying here, and besides, I don't want it. Go now."

"When can I see you again, Mare? Tomorrow?" To be thrown out of her room was as terrible as being ejected from . . . he couldn't think of it, but it was damn terrible.

"No. Not tomorrow."

"When?"

"Don't whine. I'm very busy now. The semester's almost over; I'll have to make up final exams and read a lot of papers. I won't have much time."

"But Mare." He had to come back again. He was missing her already. He loved her; she was the only one he wanted to return to.

"Get dressed. Here's your shirt. That's right. And your socks. Good."

"Please. You're all I've got now."

"In that case, my poor child, you possess very little. There now, don't fret. You're very nice and I'm sure everything will be all right. You'll see. Do you need any money?" (Catherine the Great, when she reached the age of fifty-five and Potemkin, though ten years her junior, was too old for her, took lovers in their early twenties who were first subjected to tests by ladies-in-waiting for their physical, mental and erotic suitability. When she tired of them, the Empress sent them away with kingdoms, jewels or money and the benediction of history.)[1]

"No, Mare, I want you."

She smiled at him in the mirror while brushing out her long hair. "My pet. Your eyes are lovely and your thighs

[1] Oldenbourg, Zoé, *op. cit.* P. 325.

35

are very strong. But I have no time and you must be brave."

He pouted, not knowing whether to be offended or flattered. "I almost died," he said.

"I'm sure you did," she answered absent-mindedly and pulled the hair through a rubber band.

"Would it have mattered?"

"What do you mean?" Love-making had given a nice patina to her skin, she saw with satisfaction. "Oh, if you had died, you mean." He winced. "I would have been very sorry."

"Me too. I wish I knew a lot of things."

She turned and looked at him. This was always the most difficult part, discarding them after use. He wore a shirt, tie and two socks but nothing else. "Why?"

"So I could talk to you."

She stroked the back of his head and handed him his shorts. "I'm going to the bathroom now. Make sure the lock catches when you leave." Better to do it in their apartments; then you could leave immediately afterwards. Thank God, she thought when she heard the door close, he's gone. She went back to bed, savoring the three hours of solitude she could look forward to before the psychoanalyst she had met last week would arrive.

He was alone in the foul May air, clad in a few articles of clothing and his full freedom. His stomach made a sound like the washer switching into rinse and everyone was trying to be rid of him. She was unjust, she didn't know he loved her. She had exiled him without fair trial. His hand in his pocket felt paper: the address the midget Negro had given him at lunch. No one wanted Scudley but here was a man with fantasies to sell. He had been banished but he could still dream. The fantasies were cheap, the guy had said, and Scudley was suddenly in the market for them.

36

4

At Bix (erstwhile "The Buck") Jones' place it was happening, as usual. Scudley rang the bell and waited; then again and again until it was finally answered by a large, dark man whom Scudley at first took for a pirate. He wore a black patch over one eye, red shorts, a beard, whiskers and a general air of malevolence. "Mr. Jones?" asked Scudley timorously.

"Bix. That's me. What're you?"

"Someone sent me. A little guy"—he measured the height with his open hand—"light-skinned."

"Jo-jo. A little ratmunk he is, don't you think? Scurfing around in corners, always has his nose in things. You?"

"Me? I'm John Scudley."

"So?"

"I've been killing myself. Are you Bix Jones?"

Either Scudley had hit on the password or else the pirate found sudden reasons for wanting the door closed. He clasped Scudley by the shoulders and bounced him in. "One of Jo-jo's cats," he announced as they entered the room.

At first Scudley saw only a pink haze. The air smelled sweet, a tropical jungle in an improbable springtime: smells of woman, heat, ripeness, the river. His body remembered Mare's and the sweetness jabbed him in the belly. He sat down quickly on a large cushion with tassels and gold braid. Someone handed him a marijuana cigarette. He inhaled and passed it on. Languor settled on him; he realized he was tired, hungry and very weak. The room swirled. Large flowers on velvet wallpaper, tendrils of wrought iron, a baby-faced clock, two stuffed tigers with leering emerald eyes, mirror in a gilt frame, girls with long blond hair that weaved and billowed like veils of a belly dancer, muscular dark hands, large teeth, odds and ends of things, toes, erections under trousers, thick ankles . . . he puffed again, took too much air and placed both hands on the floor to quiet it.

". . . it was a groove, man."

The blonde girl he was speaking to leaned back, thighs apart, a limp hand trailing his shoulders. "Shake it, baby," she ordered in a harsh whisper. Her grated voice, Scudley realized, was trying to follow the record:

> Make it,
> break it,
> shake it all around . . .

"You got any food?" Scudley asked plaintively, catching the ankles nearest him and looking up.

Bix laughed. "Listen to the man! Charley here wants some food. Hey, Foots, bring Charley some cheese if we got any. And ham. I saw a great fucking ham there this morning. You like ham, Charley?"

"John," said John Scudley.

Still laughing, Bix ruffled his hair and squashed Scudley's hand on his way across the room. Scudley didn't complain. He sighed and closed his eyes. Woman smell, deep, loving armpits, caressing heat and you could drift off, sleep, your head in the lap of some woman, mothered to death by her thighs and smell.

"Is this Charley yours?" asked Bix.

Jo-jo squealed and made a quick leap in the air. "Fantasy! He's the fantasy-man. Asked me if I had any fantasies at the diner. Told him I knew where to find them. Isn't that gorgeous? Fantasies!"

"One of those, huh," said Bix thoughtfully. "You're out of your mothering mind, Jo-jo, picking up any Charley you meet. One day it'll be fuzz and we'll all be busted on account of you."

Jo-jo simpered. "I'm hungry," said Scudley.

"You mean that mothering bastard didn't bring no cheese? Foots! you fuck-up. I said cheese. And ham. Now."

Foots came quickly and Bix slapped him across the face. "Here's your food, mister," he told Scudley and handed it to him. He watched while Scudley ate and then, crouching on his knees, brought his mouth to Scudley's ear. "You want to see them fantasies? Wait a while, I got lots, so long as you got bread. Just make the scene a while, baby, then we'll talk."

Scudley nodded. The food made him feel better and he was becoming accustomed to the smell. People danced, juggled, climbed the air, clawed at it, contracted their stomachs, threw out their groins. Tiny skirts held in quivering thighs. Short hair, long hair, o my beard and whiskers said the rabbit, a terrible hurry, faces go funny, dark glasses (the better to see you with, my dear), thumping buttocks, quick! down the rabbit hole. You had to move as fast as you could to stay where you were. What happiness! He felt quite at home here with these bright, indistinguishable containers bouncing away. Like cocktail shakers, they mixed things together for greater potency and quicker oblivion.

"You there," someone called. "Come on, baby, make it."

Scudley shook his head, smiled and with prodigious effort managed to stand up. He was taken into a ring of dancers, each transfixed in syncopated hypnosis, jerking his body as though strings were attached to each joint. Scudley frugged with the rest of them; awkwardly at first and then the muted light, the heat, noise and smell combined to drug him. He was high, he was flying, he forgot his body, no longer had a sense of belonging to it; arms, legs, torso

moved of their own accord, sweat blinded him a moment
and then was wiped away by a pale hand he had seen
before; the floor disappeared, rose up to the ceiling, fused
with the wall; he flew over obstacles; this marionette was
possessed of miraculous dexterity, suppleness, could never
fall or stub its toes and he gyrated even faster, throwing out
arms, climbing an invisible ladder up to the skies. At the
end, he fell on a couch and warm, welcome hands soothed
him. He opened his eyes and met a pair of very dark, very
friendly ones smiling at him. The girl wore no make-up, her
head looked as though a wig of pubic hair had been placed
on it. "You were beautiful, baby," she told him, without
coquetry.

"White," he breathed, "you should be in white. Sister of
mercy, you shouldn't be here."

She looked at him thoughtfully. "You can see that, can
you? You're right, you're right, you milk-fed atheist. I
belonged to the F.O.I.; I was Louisa X. But when they
killed Brother Malcolm I couldn't believe in them any
more." She sighed. "All that violence. It bugs me now; I've
had it. I want to marry a pale-skinned man and live in a
ranch-type house. Though of course," she added hastily,
remembering he was white, "Muhammed is a good man.
He's well-meaning, you know, for a mystic. But some kind of
health nut, eating one meal in three days. Man doesn't live
by absence of bread alone," she said sadly. "Even the best
nuts are no use now. We've got to crack the system." She
sighed again and moved away from him. Her head rested
against the wall; her hands were folded on her lap and her
feet crossed. Scudley thought she was an angel; he never
wanted her to stop.

"What's F.O.I.?" he asked.

She opened her eyes wide and gave him a long, mournful
look. "Oh, man! You don't even know that?" She closed
them again. "Maybe I'm wrong; it's people like you need

to be exploded out. We've got to stick fireworks up you where it hurts till you're bombed out of your mind, till you know what Jonah felt like when the whale spat him out."

Strapped to a skyrocket or missile, moving up with the speed of light, ripping through clouds, the atmosphere, into an icy world of incompleted air, stars, large hydrogen atoms. Oh, her words were music so sweet that his eyes filled with tears. Exploded out and up, riding a firecracker, sparklers in the eyes, round and round the Catherine wheels, crashing into a meteor and splattering to earth in showers of light and color, Roman candles bursting in air, gave proof through the night . . . "Move me, baby." His dark angel looked avenging now. She pulled him to his feet, put her arms around his neck and swayed against him.

> Let me tell you, babe,
> You must be dreamin'.
> The world ain't spinnin'
> Just for you alone. . . .

She rubbed against him, pussy fur electrified by dog hair, and the heat was intolerable. He was afraid of passing out and clung tightly to her for support.

"C'mon, girl. Whatcha doing to Whitey?" Bix carried her off and the two of them danced in a far corner, frozen, despite the heat, into a courtly masque.

> . . . the world is rough, babe,
> Out there on your own.

How true, thought Scudley and felt sorry for himself again. Here, too, in this underbelly of night, no one wanted him. Maybe they all had a secret he wasn't allowed to share.

"You want to take a trip?" asked Foots.

How kind, thought Scudley, he wants me with him. He nodded happily. But before Foots had taken him away, Louisa intercepted them. "Where you going, Foots?"

"On a trip."

41

"You taking him with you?"

"Yeah. It's all right. We got lots of the shit."

"I wasn't thinking of that. You there, you know what you're doing?"

"Taking a trip with Foots," answered Scudley. Everyone was kind; he had only to surrender himself to them and the secret would be shared.

"You know what that means?" she asked impatiently.

He looked blank. "Oh, you baby!" She laughed. "Hey, Foots, he thought maybe you were taking him to Paris. You ever heard of L.S.D., baby, seeing how you're so unfamiliar with initials?"

"Sure, I've heard of it." Many magazines had carried long articles on the subject recently; the one in *Life* had beautiful pictures. He'd read it as soon as it came in, before putting it on the stand. He'd learned to take such care in reading magazines that no one could tell they had even been touched.

"Lysergic acid diethylamide. Man, you're gorgeous. You're something else. Take care of him, Foots, we'll need him for the Christmas show at All Saints'—the little lamb going to slaughter." Then, taking him by the shoulders and shaking him, she said with anger, "Stop horsing around. Use your brain, if you got any. You don't just drift along with this shit. Take it if you want but Jesus Christ, boy, at least make believe you're conscious. You people!" She almost spat. "It's always the same. How long you going to let dumbness guide you?" She threw him off and he fell into the arms of Foots. "Take him," she said contemptuously. "Out of his mind might be the best place for him to go." But Foots pushed him back down on the cushion and went off alone.

"Anything wrong?" asked Jo-jo.

"They won't let me take a trip."

"Don't feel too down, man, you still got your fantasies."

"Yeah," he said, unconvinced. What was Mare doing

now? Nobody understood him. Why did they bother talking to him at all? If they'd only leave him in peace, let him do what he was used to doing, everything would be all right. His fatal mistake, he told himself, was taking those Seconals. Trying to be like everyone else. If you die the way everyone does, you have to live that way, too. He should have tried the poisoned oysters, or drowned himself in the bathtub like he did the first time. Even falling from a window was better, but if you just drugged yourself the way everyone did, you had to take the consequences. When the reefer came around this time, he kept it.

A flash of gold spun crazily and a monkey was sitting on its tail. Into the back room, oozing turpentine like sweat, through the long tunnel into the soft, furry basket with jingle bells. He laughed; it tickled. It tickled him very much and he couldn't stop laughing. The tickling went on too long, he squirmed away from it, the tickling wouldn't stop, laughter became painful, he subsided into giggles, then another wave rose and pulled him up with it, up into more laughter, shrieks and the sound was bouncing off the walls, hitting him like a boomerang in the head, the stomach—a small, fuzzy mammal, snout shivering and sniffing the air. Mushrooms in a wet forest, squish, squash, how funny, that sound of murdering mushrooms, mooing, mushy; and now oops, up they went, the whole forestful, a faggot of mushrooms taking off to the sky. Pow! Superman lands on them and they explode, erupt, sparklers first and then a great cloud, the whole world covered by mushrooms, everything dinky, musty, swallowed in mushroom smell, vapor spreading, no way to get out, no exit, drowning in mushrooms, nothing left to breathe . . . "I've got him," said a voice. "What do we do now? Can't throw him out like this."

"Make him puke."

Up it came, by the roots, from deep below ground, rocks, moss, worms, bugs, things that go bump in the night,

43

great hairy stems and wortles all rose, the forest became a sea of mushroom, closer to breaking point, needles of the evergreen tickled his throat, toadstools pressed against his larynx and then flood, explosion, tempest and the cool green eye. He smiled up feebly from the bathroom floor and someone—not ungently—was mopping him up, sweeping him into little piles, gathering them together, then scrubbing, scraping, polishing until he rose to his feet, sparkling new and dazzling bright, radiance upon him, wings sprouting from his back. Beatitude of regurgitation. The pure soul, like a freshly starched shirt, lay waiting to be claimed.

Two hours later Scudley was feeling very tranquil and Bix promised him that soon now they'd get down to fantasies. Time had long ago vanished, been pulled out like taffy until there was nothing left and, though doors were continually opening and closing, Scudley couldn't tell whether people were leaving or arriving. The volume of humans seemed to remain constant; Bix, Louisa, Foots and Jo-jo were all still there. The heat was ebbing, the smell had grown fainter and noise was more modulated. Everyone seemed to be just as contented as Scudley; tranquillity ruled, over all heads was peace, everyone moved on swells of time, not caring about direction. A slim girl with enormous gray eyes (Scudley could now see clearly in the half-lighted room) entered and looked familiar. She hugged Bix and greeted the inmates of the room with small flourishes before coming over to Scudley. "I know you," she said. "You work in my father's store, don't you? And you won't tell him, will you?"

"Tell him what?"

"That I was here. He's so, so, well—you know him."

"Yes." He nodded wisely. This, then, was Molly MacGrogan; appetizing and about eighteen. He liked the thought of entering a conspiracy with her; but then, as had so often happened in the past few days, his stomach, though empty, went through the cycle of a washing machine. "Blp" was all he could say, and then: "Bleesch."

She agreed, settled down next to him and accepted a reefer. "I used to go with Jack over there," she confided, jerking her head in the direction of the two stuffed tigers, "and I sort of stuck with the scene. Dad doesn't know about it, didn't know about Jack—he's funny that way. Should be on the White Citizens' Council or something. I mean, he's not a bad man, but so *dense*. Prejudiced, you know."

"Gluk gluk." He wanted to embrace her. He pressed her hand very hard and the cycle stopped. "Your dad fired me today."

"He did? How awful. Why?"

"I committed suicide again."

Her eyes opened very wide until the black rings of her corneas were encircled with white. She spoke breathlessly: "You did? You often do that?"

"Seven times in five years," he said nonchalantly, to coax her admiration.

"How'd you do it? Pistol? Slitting your wrists? Or did you"—her voice quavered—"hang yourself?"

He was ashamed. "Pills."

"Oh. Just pills."

"But other times I didn't take pills. I once fell on my sword."

"Really?"

Not really, but Scudley hadn't the heart to tell her. She was so young, so innocent and seemed to have no idea of the difficulties involved in killing oneself. He'd never tried anything heroic. Usually, he sought death through ingestion—poison, the insides of beetles, contaminated water, combinations of food guaranteed to be fatal—and once he'd simply buried himself in a large snowdrift when the temperature was fifteen below. He was a failure and a fake. He could do nothing with himself, not even turn himself into a corpse. But it really *was* difficult to kill oneself painlessly, he rationalized, and Scudley had a horror of pain. And yet, a vision sustained him, a vision of the final, the successful attempt with the ultimate, glorious plunge to death. He and a beautiful woman riding in a silver convertible, both slightly sunburnt, she smelling of Russian leather in a pastel-colored dress with a lime rickey in her hand, another held in place on the dashboard for him. The sun was slowly sinking behind the ocean, spreading fingers of rose, yellow, chartreuse, lilac, gold, turquoise and amber. The sky flamed with more brilliant hues, too glorious to be looked at with the naked eye. They were both wearing sunglasses, her frame thicker than his; her hand was very soft and her nails glistened with frosted polish. The radio blared an old song, "Mood Indigo" perhaps, or "Blue Moon":

> And when I looked, the moon had turned
>   to gold
> Blue-ue-ue moon,
> Now I'm no longer alone,
> Without a dream in my heart,
> Without a love of my own . . .

and they exhaled pale, mother-of-pearl smoke from their menthol-fresh lungs. The car sped faster and faster towards the sunset, a kaleidoscope where moon and sun embraced, stars glittered and splintered, the speedometer was at 120 and going up, higher and higher, voices singing, skin smarting, 160, 180, 200 and colors fused to white, their bodies melted, he let go the wheel and gathered her in his arms. . . . But Scudley hardly knew how to drive and the road to paradise would require many lessons.

"You've got lots of courage," she told him. "I'd never dare do that. When I think of it—but no, it's blasphemy, you know? Killing yourself. But these queer feelings come over me sometimes; I think how nice it would be to kill myself and other people, too. Especially children, they're so juicy."

A sleepy voice nearby said distinctly: " 'All things have a Mother/ And she has a name.' The Tao Tĕ Ching. Don't go throwing your Zen around at me, boy. We've had that scene. Lao-tzu anyday."

Molly's hand lay softly but affectionately in Scudley's. Her voice scampered on, a strange little savage misplaced somewhere behind the gold cross round her neck: "You munch crunch on their bones and I think I'm a kind of mystic. I see things other people don't see. Jack once said I could be a saint. Saint Molly, can you imagine! I see the entrails of things, all rosy and purple, glistening over everything and inside's the heart, like an embryo's heart, pumping in and out, just a speck really and the whole thing is beautiful, a painting, with those long tubes crawling around like giant worms, only better and moving in and out and you can see them going on and on, a long, long line around the earth and then crushing it, smothering the earth to death while the serpentseaedslithering . . ." Scudley could no longer follow what she was saying. This girl put the fear of death in him—what was he thinking? Still, she was such a pretty little thing. Nice to have around the house, while her father fumed among the sawdust. What would Mare say? Would Mare care? Would he dare? Mare, care, dare—it was time for the fantasies.

A creature with the body of a twelve-year-old girl and the head of a witch was lying dead on her side while a goat nuzzled her pubic hair and an enormous offspring of man and gorilla was entering her anus. This was the third picture of the present series, which combined necrophilia and child molestation. They had already covered homosexuality (with interesting permutations, a pyramid effect: one woman at the center, one sucking at her breasts, the other at her genitals, each of them being penetrated by a man who in turn was being buggered by another man), sadism, masochism and flagellation. The only thing to be said in favor of these photographs was their absolute lack of racial discrimination. Scudley had reacted to the first batch with nausea and was feeling sicker by the minute. A woman with an artificial penis strapped to her was masturbating while a man licked her from behind. Here, the flesh of an old back came away in strips and brass knuckles ground into the belly. His skin crawled with lice, spiders, tarantulas. He couldn't look any more; this last series was the worst of them. And then there was more, Scudley only half-aware of the themes: incest, sodomy and a variety of fetishes, ending in excreta. A woman shitting into the open mouth of a man. He was numb by now and when it was all finished, Scudley mechanically counted out twenty dollars, gave them to Bix and left the room like a sleepwalker. He felt nothing, no disgust, no emotion at all; his marrow had been removed along with his organs. Nothing in his life had prepared him for the viewing of these pictures and, like most who come unprepared to an experience, he let the events occur without participating in them. He was a thing, with nothing to do but be.[1]

When he entered the next room, Molly rushed to him, weaving slightly. "Where'd you go, Johnny? I want to hear more about your fantasies."

The word was an electric current, effecting shock treatment. His eyes clouded with grief, he trembled. "Don't say that, don't ever say that. Those things are dirty, they're evil. No one should have fantasies, they're full of filth." He took her by the hand and pulled her away but she freed herself and ran back to the couch. Alone, Scudley walked down the hall, found the door in the darkness, opened it and walked

[1] Cf. Sade, Marquis de, *The complete Justine, Philosophy in the Bedroom, and other writings*, compiled and translated by Richard Seaver and Austryn Wainhouse. Grove Press. New York, 1965. *Passim.*

out into the murky dawn like the survivor of a shipwreck making his first foray on the island which saved him from death but which may contain deaths far more horrible than drowning.

5

As so often happens when one thinks of the devil, he appears. Marya and Father Niemans met head-on in the intersection between spices and detergents. Marya pulled back her cart. "Don't they feed you at the monastery?" she asked sweetly. She had on a jersey dress of muted orange with Mexican-style embroidery of royal blue and yellow. Her ears were studded with tiny pearls, her hair was freshly washed and perfumed.

"Of course, of course. This is just for my sister. . . ."

"Is she married?"

"Yes. Two boys."

She tried to imagine him in a family setting: television on, toys scattered over the floor, dirty dishes, a frumpled housewife with faded hair, the beery husband dozing and belching in an armchair. Seated among them, a man of God who drank his beer and watched the fight, calling to the children every now and then to be more quiet. She was glad she looked good; she had deliberated whether or not to do the shopping in curlers and in the end nothing more than a whim had made her decide to adorn herself for the supermarket. "We meet so soon. Would you call it fate, Father, or the will of God?" She blushed slightly, in case she was being blasphemous.

Father Niemans smiled. "I'd call it happy circumstance. How's your work going?"

She could feel the eyes of other customers on them and

50

pushed out her breasts while holding in her stomach. Handsome young priest and voluptuous woman. There was a novel in it somewhere, or perhaps a Broadway musical. "Oh, there's always a lot to do at the end of the semester, but things seem to be under control." This morning she had written out the essay question for the Pope-Johnson exam: "Lady Montagu wrote a series of essays entitled 'The Nonsense of Common-Sense.' To what extent do you think nonsense entered into England's Age of Reason? Give examples." The Freshman English exam would have to be divided into two parts; she had been the one to suggest that linguistics be taught along with literature. And then the seminar on Class Struggles in Western Literature—she'd had a hard time getting the department to accept that course and it probably hadn't been worthwhile. One semester wasn't long enough to teach her students what class struggle meant and she had been forced to confine the reading list to revolutionary works. Next year she would teach The Novel as Middle-Class Literature, but she would have to include Dickens, and the edition she owned, in twenty-five volumes, contained such small print that she was already weary. "And you, Father? Still continuing your hospital rounds?"

"Another week."

They walked along the aisles together, pushing their carts in front of them. "Special Today—3 for $1.00," "5¢ off," "The Quality Food," "Mrs. Rappaport's Pickles—Guaranteed Kosher," "Fresh Today," "Mother's Tuna." "I've memorized the Creed," she said.

"Already?"

A blur of condiments: relish, ketchup, piccalilli, chutney, mustard, Diabolo sauce, A-1, barbecue sauce, soy sauce, tartar sauce . . . "I believe in God, the Father Almighty," she began softly, "Creator of heaven and earth; and in Jesus Christ, His only Son, our Lord." Now past the cookies and crackers, chocolate-covered marshallows, sesame crackers, cream sandwiches, wheat, rye, pumpernickel, saltines, animal crackers, muffins, rolls, cheese crackers, grahams, chocolate chip, mint, coconut, oatmeal, lemon . . . "Who was conceived by the Holy Ghost, born of the Virgin Mary, suffered under Pontius Pilate, was crucified, died, and was buried." Beer in mugs, bottles, cans, from Denmark, Holland, Mexico, Germany, Milwaukee, the 2000-year-old Brewmaster who had seen it all, was there at the beginning, using rocks in place of footballs, a friend of Shakespeare, dweller in caves, connoisseur of women, who was there at the beginning and never changed, eternal life in his frothy beer . . . "He descended into hell; the third day He arose again from the dead; He ascended into heaven, sitteth at the right hand of God, the Father Almighty: from thence He shall come to judge the living and the dead." The cereals were most lively. Get a rousing start, Begin Your Day with Energy, SelectaPak for discriminating children, crackle, puff, flake, chip, ball, square, cross, with instant banana, dehydrated dust turns to fruit . . . "I believe in the Holy Ghost," free war set for your child, complete with wounds, eye patches, bandages, splints, crutches, bullets, stretchers, guns, tanks, nuclear bombs . . . "the holy Catholic Church," life-size little girl doll with hair that can be shampooed, set, bleached and permanent waved. Comes complete with necessary chemicals, dryer, three wigs, curlers, rubber gloves, only $10.00 with box top from any one of . . . "the communion of saints, the forgiveness of sins," the deep arsenal of frozen foods: berries, vegetables, mashed potatoes, pizza, coffeecake, blueberry turnovers, *croissants*, soft-shell crabs, South African lobster tails, nourishment is frozen solid, chicken hard enough to crack a skull, strawberry shortcake, knishes, Danish, cream puffs, éclairs, as he eats so shall he be judged, brownies, doughnuts, waffles, pineapple upside-down cake, have we not power to eat and drink?, lemon meringue pie, deep-frozen belly, sweetness, in

52

the day that thou eatest thereof thou shalt surely die, mince pie, apple strudel . . . "the resurrection of the body, and life everlasting."

"Amen," said Father Niemans. "Very good. We can start with the catechism on Monday." They walked in silence a few minutes, each selecting what he had come to buy. The belly and the mouth; food and words; Marya was feeling very spiritual. "Have you seen John Scudley?" asked the priest. He could smell her perfume and tried to widen the distance between them but the aisle was narrow and the aroma strong.

"Briefly."

"The poor man." That sympathy was too easy, too professional, she thought, but when she looked at him she saw that his forehead was wrinkled and sadness dragged at the rims of his eyes. Amazing. Priestly compassion was an occupational hazard, but this young man seemed worried, thoughtful, as though John Scudley had opened up a new page of suffering or loneliness which he was trying hard to read despite failing eyesight. She wanted to touch his hand but didn't dare. "You seem to care a lot."

"A man who wants to take his life . . . Despair . . ."

"The only sin."

He looked at her with surprise. "Yes." What was this creature anyway? Perhaps she had been sent to him for deeper reasons than he suspected; perhaps she was not there merely to tempt him (he had imagined the writhings, the agony, the cry in the night: Lord make me chaste, but not yet) but also to be led by him out of darkness.

That's the only sin, she thought, and that's why frivolity is grace, even if it can lead to hysteria. He was thinking: Faith. . . . The hemline of her dress brushed against him; he wondered if she and Scudley . . . Faith. And he closed his eyes a moment.

They went through the cashier's line together and then

parted. Pushing her cart to her Triumph, Marya thought of Johnson, Swift and Sterne; all of them mad or terrified. The old Watchmaker scared them into their reasonable wits. Sense was the only way to conquer sensibility, drunk for a penny, dead drunk for tuppence[1] and only the sparkle of wit could scare off the willies. She smiled lovingly at them, unloading her groceries. To the inmates of Fleet Street she extended her condolences and taught them the modern, feminine application of their heretical *bon mot:* Sex does more than Jesus can/ To justify God's ways to man.[2] She had no doubt that they were listening to her. She was on intimate terms with them all; they had left her their compliments in verse and prose and, though circumstances prevented her from reciprocating with warm beer or a warm bed, she sent them affectionate messages now and then, gossip or epithets about men and manners in the present time.

When she arrived home, the phone was ringing. "Mare," the voice bleated, "it's me. I feel awful."

"You should have gone right to bed after the hospital." She decided not to tell him that she'd just met Father Niemans. "Does your stomach hurt?"

"Everything does. I can't sleep. I want to see you."

"That's impossible. Take an aspirin or Seconal—oh, sorry—and go to sleep. You'll feel better after a nap."

"I didn't sleep at all last night. I don't want to sleep. I get dreams."

[1] See footnote 2 on p. 16.
[2] See Housman, A. E. (1859–1936). In "The Day of Battle" (included in *A Shropshire Lad*) are the lines:

> Oh many a peer of England brews
> Livelier liquor than the Muse,
> And malt does more than Milton can
> To justify God's ways to man.

This is, of course, a parody of Milton's expressed purpose (in Book I, line 26 of *Paradise Lost*) to "justify the ways of God to men."

"Of course you do. Everyone does. It's a necessary phase in the REM cycle."

"REM?" he said dubiously, but, remembering his inadequacy in coping with initials, didn't dare ask what the letters stood for.

"Rapid Eye Movements; it comes after stage four, Delta, when sleep is deepest."

"Oh." The information made him curiously despondent and very lonely. "Won't you come to the delta with me?" lamented something inside him. "Mare, it's these nightmares. Huge lizards and things with no heads and you touch something and it falls off, the skin I mean, or a leg or an eye pops out. Oh see me, please. Mare, you got to."

"Can't." When she replaced the receiver, Marya also felt lonely. Tonight she would make herself dinner and go over student papers. She, whose hair was freshly set, who had sprayed cologne over her whole body and between her toes, who had spent twenty minutes in making up and whose new dress suited her magnificently, would be sitting alone with typing errors. But then, would wasting time with Scudley be any better? She was cast in the mold of greatness; she had not been created for silly men and tedium. She was too beautiful for Scudley, too opulent; a gift too great for him even to understand. He had neither talent nor training to appreciate her properly. Yesterday he had pleased her, but that was yesterday and she had taken no pains about her appearance for his sake. Beautiful, intelligent, sensual, she, Marya Poum, who had been loved by many, was now slowly expiring among words, which could never send her flowers, couldn't kill themselves for her or bequeath her more power than she already possessed. Men were as easy to find as worms under a rock, but if you took them for more than toys, you were sure to be disappointed. They didn't love you well enough and, what was far, far worse, didn't allow you to love them the way you wanted. They shrank from love as if too much of it were a perversion; they ran away when you tried to give yourself to them or to love or to heroism. They didn't leave you free to expostulate in the grand style. Perhaps a priest . . . he believed in holy passion, in the sanctity of love. He had given himself to God and must be able to accept love intense enough to blind or strike him dead. This myth of masculinity that men are heirs to! All it does is make them into turtles. Hard shell, sure, but they'd all been overexposed to Hollywood and Marlboro ads and thought that a real man was always invulnerable. But a priest wasn't really a man, though he could probably become one and then, backed by the whole hierarchy, the popes, saints and the marching church militant, he would bring love with a sword and perform miracles. If he would bring to her all the power he represented, she could then become his thing.

At nine-thirty that evening, Marya developed cramps of nausea whenever she came across "essence," "nature," "sensibility" or "objective correlative" and went out for a drive. The top was down and, though she felt chilly, she wanted the wind whipping against her. She dodged in and out among the cars, playing her favorite game of "bullfighter"—to come within an inch of catastrophe and then suddenly swerve. On the open road, she pressed the accelerator until she was going seventy-five. After a few minutes the flashing red light on the car behind signaled her to pull over.

She had a technique with cops, finely perfected through years of experience. It was simple: the cop came over, saw you were a woman and expected tears, flirtation or arguments. You offered none of those; you handed him your license and registration without looking up and then, while he was examining them, lit a cigarette. He would say, "Do you realize you were going seventy-five?"

"Yes"—in a bored voice.

"Forty miles above the speed limit?"

56

"Yes."

"Why were you speeding?"

(Here Marya had given a variety of answers: "I simply wanted to," "I was in a hurry," "I enjoy fast driving," "The day is beautiful" and once, "Because I'm drunk.")

"Don't you know it's dangerous?"

"Perhaps." The important thing was never to look at him. If you happened to glance in his direction, you could never raise your eyes higher than his belt. At this point his bewilderment would begin to frustrate him; he was accustomed to every kind of bribery, but bored indifference, especially from a woman, made him uneasy. He hadn't yet decided whether you were very rich, the police commissioner's sister, or some kind of nut. His curiosity was roused, he would now do anything to have you look at him, to have you acknowledge his existence at least, since you were incompetent to recognize his authority.

"If I let you go this time . . ." And he would wait, tensely, for a smile or expression of relief. No response—it was vital, at this point, to resist any urge to say or do something.

"Would you promise not to speed again?"

"No, officer"—now you could look deep in his eyes with a smile either friendly or provocative—"I can't promise that. I was careless, I didn't see your car in the mirror. If I had, I would certainly have slowed down."

You were putting him on, perhaps, but you were all right; he could see that. And now began the hard work (but worth it—the $15.00 could be paid, but convictions were marked on your license, and after three it would be revoked) of talking to the policeman, having a cigarette or perhaps a drink with him, allowing him to take your phone number, listening to his problems, his theories, stories from his childhood and anecdotes about his profession. The whole process sometimes took two hours, but Marya had never in her life been convicted for speeding. And the encounters could be pleasant or funny—two cops, on different occasions, had quoted the Prologue to the *Canterbury Tales* in Middle English; one had given her a Russian lesson; a young man, in his first month of duty, had discussed the question of capital punishment with her, saying, "I agree with Camus on that— if one innocent man's been killed, the whole system's got to be abolished." (Just her luck, she had thought at the time; anyone else would have met a brutal, dumb fascist— precisely what she hoped to get when she took the car over sixty in a hospital zone—while she had to meet a boy who read Camus and wrote poetry in his spare time.) He was a cop, he said, instead of a poet, because, "You can do some good this way. If I save one baby, that's worth more'n a hundred poems."

This one, she saw in her rear-view mirror, was her type: tall, broadly built and in his twenties. She had her papers ready and the window down by the time he came over. When they entered the conversation stage, he had accepted her cigarette and was sitting beside her in the car. His eyes were very blue, he was fair and his chin ended brutally in a clean line. He clenched his jaw whenever he was silent and the bone strained through his close-shaven cheek. The bottom joints of his thumbs jutted out like enormous marbles and in his eyes were slivers of metal. She was fascinated; she wanted to melt down those pieces of steel into a rich liquid. His voice was guttural, his alveopalatals fused to a single voiced explosive stop. She smiled, nodded, shook her head in sympathy or disbelief and her show of interest had the effect she planned. He stroked her arm, leaned closer and his left thigh sat heavily on the leather, an enormous piece of meat, packaged in navy blue and quivering. Everywhere, his flesh was in revolt against its bonds. The veins of his neck stood out over the collar and below his belt he strained to burst the clothing. He enchanted her; she couldn't take her eyes away from him; the red light continued flashing and she relaxed in a tense, expectant surrender. Then came lucidity and she told him he was an officer on duty, he might be needed somewhere now. He considered what she said, gave a hopeless, assenting shrug and then sat up abruptly as inspiration hit him. "You come to my car. We can sit there and—and talk and I can hear the radio if anything's on."

She cocked her head in mock demurral. "Aw, come on, baby. It's the same thing, isn't it? If I sit here or you sit there?"

"Well . . ." She wanted this scene to continue. In high school, she hadn't gone out with boys. She wanted that courtship and coyness, the adolescent American version of the chivalric code. But she was thirty-two and his lips were half-open, the thick tongue showing between the cleft. "O.K. But not for long."

He grinned, patted her hand, jumped out and with extraordinary speed was opening her door, assisting her with an arm somewhere between her waist and breasts. In his car, he extinguished the flashing beacon but left on the headlights. It was something like a Pontiac, she judged, a heavy car that meant business and got straight to the point. The police radio went on and off abruptly, sometimes as incomprehensible as an airport loud-speaker, then lapsing into chatty small talk as though one were listening in on a party line. "Does it have to be so loud?"

"Afraid so, baby. Come here." Aggressively, he pulled her towards him so that she lay sprawled across his chest, her face partly smothered in the uniform. "Ninth and Main. Are you there, 527? False alarm, I think. Same boys down there two nights ago. The Italian kid and his pal, a Dago, too. They might've gone down Pine or Thachery." She dog paddled to surface. "How do they know," she asked, "who sent in that false alarm? Or even if it is one? How

59

can you accuse someone before the crime is even identified?"

"Easy, baby, you got a long slide home," he said, stroking her hair as if it were made of glass and his hand were a mallet. "Nobody's gonna get in trouble. You been reading too much about police brutality and all that. I been in five years now and never seen any. You know what the guys down't station house do when someone's brought in? They ask him if he wants a hamburger. If he does, they bring it to him, with ketchup and relish. And a Coke."

She didn't answer, partly because she had no grounds for either believing or not believing him, and partly because his easygoing pleasantness annoyed her. Only in Europe had she met true fascists, with whom her liberal views could serve as piquant provocation to a form of rape. There was no point at all in arguing with nice American boys who happened to be Republicans instead of Democrats or from the South instead of the North. His right arm was hanging around her neck, fingers dangling a few inches from her nipples. Stealthily, the hand crawled to the V of her neckline and fanned her skin with such delicacy that she couldn't tell whether he was actually touching her or only the air a few millimeters away. She became totally passive, her nerves moving closer to her skin while his caresses grew stronger and lower until his fingers found the cleavage between her breasts and buried themselves inside. "Sol, you got a minute? Take this to Inspector Brogan. Yeah, O.K. And bring me a coffee when you came back. Black, two lumps." The left hand took hold of her nape and pulled her face to his. He kissed her softly, licked the inside of her lips, bore down with such force that her teeth tingled, and then released her. His pistol rubbed against her pelvis. "Is it loaded?" she asked. "What? The automatic? Yeah." He beamed his pride and fingered the gun. "Don't worry. The safety catch's on." She drew back his jacket and examined

60

the belt: heavy silver cartridges, each held in place by a leather strap, a row of dull, gleaming teeth above his groin. Near the heart, a shoulder holster and another gun. "Semi-automatic," he explained, "thirty-eight caliber. I got a third, too, but that's secret." He wanted to unstrap his belt but she restrained him. The hard metallic bulge felt wonderful. At her hip, unseen, it excited her; she wanted to touch it, to fondle it. Brass knuckles and a night stick, where were they? And in the glove compartment or maybe under the seat, what treasures lurked of poison gas or smoke screens or perhaps long rifles? The windows must be bullet-proof. She had so often imagined this scene—copulating with a man who was fully armed, a cop with loaded guns and ammunition—that now her eyes became moist and gratitude welled into eroticism. She licked her lips (they felt swollen already) and turned to him, breathing heavily. The hand caught her again, smashed her mouth down on his teeth and pulled her hairs so viciously that her neck jerked back. The other hand jumped out from its hiding place, made a cup around her breast, squeezed hard and jetted down, landing between her thighs like a rock. "Ow," she screamed. He silenced her with his teeth almost as Philomela was silenced. One of her arms was pinned behind his back and the lower part of it began to feel cold where the circulation was cut off. She brought her other arm from around his neck and tried to push away the hand that was grinding into her like a pestle in a mortar. "Don't," he said and fell on her, his teeth cutting her mouth, his torso flattening her against the back of the seat, the silver bullets pressing on her stomach. She thought she was suffocating; the pressure on her lungs was unbearable and only when he eased up for a moment did she recognize that the hand was still pounding her pubic bone. Bloody fool, she thought, doesn't even know where it is. But she made no effort to show him or to arrange herself in such a way that he would

61

find the clitoris by himself. With his indiscriminate force, he'd probably knock it off. "Cliff? Cliff, you there? Cliff, 349, you'd better get to old Mrs. Shubert's house. On Lindon Street"—the word startled her, as though it were the name of a dead friend—"Number 32, I think—illegal entrance and burglary. Might still be around. We don't know if he's armed. The old lady kept talking about a gun, but I doubt it. Still, don't take any chances. Prepare to shoot."

He unzipped his fly and laid his heavy penis on her clean new dress. He forced her hand to it. She held on a few moments as though gripping an iron bar. "Kiss it," he ordered, pushing down her head. "Cliff? Never mind, we got the guy. He just walked in. Maybe you better check anyway. Calm the old lady down." Tears came to her eyes; she was choking but the hand kept her there. She was gagging, drowning, she felt vomit at the back of her mouth, she couldn't hold it back any more and then, miraculously, he picked her head up gently and kissed her eyes. The hand went under her skirt, pushed back her underpants and rubbed. "Hey, Cliff! False alarm, just some punk wanting to confess. You better get down there pronto." She gasped, her eyes flew open, she stared at his smug, idiotic face and she couldn't control it, she started, she tried to stop herself, she began, she put out her leg, she tried to think of . . . but it was hopeless, useless and she was coming on his hand. "Two eighty-three? Jewelry store, 28 Main. Alarm's gone off." Nonchalantly, he licked his fingers and picked up the microphone with his other hand. "Two eighty-three. Be right there." She looked at him with intense hatred and smiled tenderly. "Two eighty-three, where are you now?"

"Around Dover and Sixth." He switched on the ignition. "Sorry, honey, I gotta go now. See you around." She adjusted her underpants, pulled down her dress and left. They waved to each other. The flashing beacon was on, the motor purred, his acceleration was really astonishing and he zoomed off, sirens wailing and then reverberating in the night. She lit a cigarette before inserting the key and sucked in deeply. It was good; the smoke assuaged her aches, massaged the battered lungs, soothed the jerky nerves. She leaned back her head and looked at the sky. If only she knew the constellations by name. The night was clear, the Big Dipper obvious, the moon at its fullest. Pale smoke floated up lazily; all sound was muted and very distant. Her hand moved over her body, which stretched and tightened under the caress. And then, with her head still thrown back, she laughed. She laughed upwards and her laughter rose up to the sky. She laughed, and the name she hurled at God increased her merriment.

6

After he spoke to Mare, Scudley remained in a simian position for hours, shoulders drooping, chin on chest, arms hanging down below his thighs. Like a satiated gorilla, he winked beside the carcass of the telephone and no thought intruded. He wanted nothing, not sleep, not food—even though he was monstrously hung-over and had eaten nothing since last night's cheese—and the extent of his desire, had he been able to formulate it, would have been to become a vegetable, be dug up from the ground, washed and frozen. A large Brussels sprout. At some point he pushed his prodigious, cabbagy self to bed. He lay flat, arms at his sides, toes pointing upwards: a fallen toy soldier. He was thinking nothing; his brain rolled wearily up and down the long tracks, growing tireder with each ascent. Then came darkness to lead him to delta.

"Are you sleeping?" a bright little voice asked. His eyes popped open to find a young girl bent over him, carefully examining his face.

"Yes," he said and the lids jumped back over the eyeballs. Nothing happened, just hallucination. No more! Life, Reality stared you in the face and you had to stare back. His eyes were closed; he slept; a dream came slithering up the ridge, trying to creep down the other side. It had horns, scales and reptilian feet. He fought with it, he pushed it back, it grew, he fought harder and finally flung it over the side. It landed on its back; bones smashed, a purple ooze

64

came up from it and Scudley cried. His hair was on fire, the flames moved down, over his eyes, his mouth, his whole body in flames, kerosene running down his cheeks, the flames leaped and someone was shaking him. "You're crying," said the young voice.

Light. That's what she'd done, turned on the god-damn light. "Off," he said and she released him. A pale-blue young woman's body stood by the bed. It folded in the middle and sat down. He touched it and found it warm. No mirage, this, just Molly MacGrogan. "Turn off the light."

She partially obeyed by switching off the overhead light and turning on the bedside lamp. "What time is it?" He would save the day and place for later questions, if he ever came to life.

"Nine-thirty."

"Morning or evening?"

"Evening."

"You're MacGrogan's daughter."

"I left."

"Was the door open?"

"Yes. That's how I came in. It was dark; I made myself a drink. You want one?"

He shook his head. "Are you staying here?"

"Please let me." She looked at him with enormous, pleading eyes and tiny sobs rippled the front of her dress. "There's a couch in there, and I wouldn't be much trouble, I promise, and I could do the cooking for you and the shopping and even clean up"—the last offer was made in a dubious tone—"and I wouldn't bug you, I promise, and I brought hardly any stuff, just a little suitcase, it's pink, and"—her eyes grew smaller and more loving—"maybe you'd like me, I mean, I'd do anything you wanted."

"You brought a suitcase?"

"Just a little one; it's pink." She seemed about to cry.

"He kicked you out?"

65

"I left," she said proudly, tossing her head and giving a slight whinny. "He's a bastard, the prejudiced old old old—popcorn"—they both looked amazed at this—"and it'd serve him right if I were black."

"And blue," he said softly and raised himself up on his elbows. "Any food in the house?"

"Spaghetti." She jumped at him with such energy that he fell back and allowed his cheeks to be licked. "I'll make some and you can have it right here, if you want, don't bother about anything."

Scudley tried to get up, but the effort was too great. He looked for a Kleenex, found an old used one under his pillow, blew into it loudly and the tissue offered no resistance. He wiped his hand on the sheet, covered the viscous glob with a pillow and threw what remained of the pink fluff under his bed. He dozed lightly, hearing her sing and talk to herself in the other room. She reappeared, carrying in her right hand a large plate piled high with spaghetti, two forks stuck into the heap like pitchforks, and with her left hand she was pouring whiskey into her mouth, looking sideways over the glass to make sure the spaghetti was still there. "Hi," she said brightly and put down the plate on the bed, its contents bouncing off in one rubbery leap. She seated herself, placed the glass at her feet and picked up the wormy bundle with both hands.

Scudley sat up, made a fist around the fork and speared. The spaghetti was cool, hard and pasty. "Beer," he said, "and butter. Garlic powder, Parmesan cheese, salt and pepper." She smiled sweetly; he ate, she drank. She picked up a long strand and dangled it like a Yo-yo. "Isn't it beautiful? Look at the way it jerks around, like it were alive or something. It looks like somebody's insides, doesn't it? Or a tapeworm." It slithered into her mouth.

Scudley realized that at last he was hungry. Manfully, plate in hand, he got off the bed and went to the kitchenette.

Molly followed him and watched with interest while he put water in the pot, dumped the spaghetti in the water, added salt and turned on the gas. "Whatcha doing?"

"Cooking dinner."

"I just did that," she explained.

"Yeah. Open a beer, will you?" the he-man ordered.

Later, in the living room in front of the television, Scudley ate enthusiastically, butter dribbling from his lips, the smell of garlic caressing his nostrils. Molly ate little; the bottle of bourbon and a small pitcher of water stood next to her and she was able, without insurmountable difficulty, to pour contents from both into her glass.

"You like drinking," Scudley observed, while sucking in a string with froglike dexterity. "It's the Irish in you."

"Not the Irish, like a fish; I like the sound of it going down."

"Whiskey makes a sound?"

"Oh yes," she explained seriously, "a very high high piping sound, not everyone can hear it, eee, scree like screeching of brakes or baby birds if they're starving and their mother's dead."

"I never knew. You think you'll be comfortable on the couch? A spring's broken."

"I've slept on worse things. A broken spring's like fall. Couch, schmouch"—she belched—"it's not where you do it, but how."

"You're kooky," he observed.

"I know," she said proudly. "You, too, that's what I like about you, you're kooky as a crippled caterpillar." She fell asleep that instant and he decided to leave her where she was. He cleared away the dishes, turned off the television and got into bed. This little creature made some of the cramps go away; the thing inside gnawing at the walls of his stomach was sleeping. She had such a soft little neck. She was like a little princess, but she talked so peculiarly.

67

Perhaps she liked goats, she certainly liked black men; she was a little witch and he'd have to figure out what to do with her. Safety begins at home. A short time later he felt something small and warm crawl in beside him and, amazingly, found himself embracing it.

"How long must you be held in the arms of the Lord before you will recognize Him as our Saviour?" The sentence pulled her out of a dream and at three in the morning the world was empty, a desert, and she, a cactus, was stuck in it alone. Nothing had happened to make her unhappy; the dream hadn't been a nightmare and she was angry at herself for feeling the way she did. Still, something gnawed at her, emptiness was smothering her, and she turned on the light.

Three in the morning is a time for conversions and defections. She was abandoned. Power and penises, young men and dictators, poetry, wit and words, all were rubbish, none made sense, and she was stranded among the gobbledygook. Marya had everything, even freedom, but there was nothing she wanted completely, nothing caught her up with such force that she could become indistinguishable from it. And so she was continually responsible, a condition not meant for humans. She had friends, made easy conquests of men, could rely on her mind and on her loyalty and could look back on accomplishments, acclaim and affairs. But the opening up of herself so many times without finding the love she hoped for (which would be the liberation from herself) brought weariness, which had no effect on her enthusiasm and showed itself only in her lack of specific desire or disappointment. Her dreams of power seemed like ambition, but there was nothing she wanted so much as to get rid of herself. The arms of the Lord were open, perhaps; if she crawled inside she might be comforted, but then again, she might be smothered.

She poured herself a glass of milk, took a pile of term

68

papers back to bed with her and was annoyed, ten minutes later, to find she was crying.

"Chick-peas and bacon rinds."

"And more than that?"

"Fried elephants' ears."

"Hey! Be serious. What do you really like most in the world?"

"Sleep."

"I mean to eat."

"You."

"Oh you're bad." She chuckled in the dark and he stroked her belly. It was small and tight. Yesterday—yesterday? yes, yesterday—Mare's voluptuous body lay across the bed and he kissed her navel. "You're like a colt, Molly."

She threw her arms around him and whinnied. "You're such a nice man, such a nice Johnny-mop."

"Go to sleep now."

"Why?"

"Because it's three o'clock in the morning."

"So what? We don't have to get up, it's Saturday, you don't have to go to work. Oh, I forgot, you don't have your job any more, do you? You don't have to get up at all."

"That's right." To sleep . . . no, damn them. Angry swirls started up in his stomach, add some bleach, let everything be white, tear off the back in strips, show them what you're here for. Too much trouble; become part of it, go along, go easy, red is the blood, white is the freedom, blue says be true: wrap that around you, so tight you don't feel anything any more. If you die of asphyxiation, so much the better. A man's a thing. . . .

"But if you're not working, what'll you do for money?"

"What'll it do for me?" She laughed. They hugged each other and fell asleep embracing, his nose and mouth buried in her hair.

* * *

69

Molly's father was snoring in the room he shared with his wife but she, in her twin bed separated from his by a rose-painted night table, was fortunately a little bit deaf and heard nothing.

Bix was stoned out of his mind and liked it that way.

In the monastery, Father Niemans was entering REM and had dreams which, happily for his soul, he would not remember.

7

After Mass, Father Niemans partook of a huge breakfast at the diner. Orange juice (large), bacon and eggs, English muffins, three cups of coffee and, as an afterthought, a cruller. Afterwards, though his hunger had no edge any more, still it persisted mildly, like chuckles following a joke long after it has been applauded by loud laughter. For two days now, he'd been constantly hungry and yet, even when he was indulging himself, was not able to commit the sin of gluttony. Contrition avoided him so long as he felt underfed and his appetite for everything from large chunks of meat to candy bars seemed unsuitable, merely, to a man who did not engage in violent physical activity. This, too, would pass; but everything he did made him conscious of food. On his hospital rounds, seeing wasted bodies and bottles of glucose slowly dripping into emaciated arms, he imagined sides of beef and pork chops. Passing movie houses, he thought of the candy and popcorn inside; at the supermarket—the Lord would have mercy—he was tempted even by the pickles. A capital sin[1]—he noticed with repugnance that he was placing the accent on "cap"—and he refrained from ordering a second cruller. Lunch was only four

[1] "Capital Sins—Offenses which, if habitual, give rise to many more sins. They are: pride, covetousness, lust, anger, gluttony, envy." Entry in the Glossary, *1966 National Catholic Almanac*. St. Anthony's Guild, Paterson, N.J. (distributed by Doubleday & Co., Garden City, N.Y.), 1966. P. 320.

71

hours away but in the hospital canteen it would be almost inedible. Perhaps on the way back to the monastery he could stop at the drugstore for a chocolate ice-cream soda. My Lord, I am not worthy.

The young waitress made out his check and smiled. Her freshly starched uniform covered her body harshly, but when she moved! When she moved, the resilient flesh underneath led its own dance. The Lord have mercy. Small hands, warm hips below the crisp, nonyielding cotton . . . I am not worthy, Lord, I am not worthy. Covetous, gluttonous, a false priest in a time-honored habit, bringing shame to the good men and saints who were clad like this in other times. I should be a mendicant; St. Francis, Holy Mary, Mother of God, show mercy on me now and in the days to come. The flesh is weak; the mind betrays; have mercy on sinners; show us the way. Quickly, under his breath, he told his rosary, Hail Mary . . . and he thought of other sinners, his brothers in the world or in Christ. We're too rich, he thought, too many temptations; St. Francis would have been fat in the affluent society. Poor countries can easily transform their citizens to saints. Anyone who hasn't eaten for three days will start to hallucinate; likewise those below the starvation threshold (six hundred calories—a steak and baked potato with sour cream). But what's to be done among ice-cream sundaes and frozen pizza and if you don't see what you want, just ask for it? Food is a central image, so is the mouth. The Word, the flesh, they will be struck dumb. . . . Take; eat; this is my body. Is the body of the Lord to be found in prebaked bread, just pop in the oven and serve? And his blood in wine like Mother used to make? Help my unbelief.[1] He tried to think of a soul in deeper agony than his own. Marya Poum . . . but his spirit had not yet been cleansed enough. John Scudley. A lonely man, tempted by damnation, brought before eternal flames

[1] St. Mark 9:23. "I do believe, Lord: help my unbelief."

through the taking in of false food. Only a Protestant, after all, but still, the man had called for a priest, for him—an unworthy witness of the True Faith, a false bearer of Good News—in his hour of need, the man had called out to be nourished at His side. Where was he now, Father Niemans wondered, and what was the shape of his soul? The police, informed by the hospital of another suicide attempt, had come to see the criminal. But Father Niemans, jealous perhaps that the law would claim jurisdiction over a sin which rightly belonged to God, or perhaps wanting to protect Scudley from the torment of questioning, had told them to go away; it had been an accident and the man was now in his care. The fat sergeant made something like a bow and, obviously relieved (there were so many of these suicide attempts nowadays, he explained to the priest), left the hospital, bequeathing the fate of John Scudley to Father Niemans. He had not been responsible. The man had been fired from his job; how was he feeling now, newly returned from the dead, with no occupation or means of livelihood awaiting him? Compare the man of God with the Son Himself, who said, "Lazarus, come forth" and he that was dead came forth.[1] How was that done? Scudley was brought back through the miracles of modern medicine and the stomach pump. What was the shape of his soul? Though he tried to resist, the good Father saw Scudley's soul appear before him: a large doughnut, raised and glazed, six for a quarter, honey dip. The doughnut was both stale and soggy, the hole narrowed and widened—now really, what was the shape of his soul?

His mind set on goodness, Father Niemans left the diner (conquering the temptation to leave an exorbitant tip) and walked resolutely to the supermarket. There, he was forced to wait ten minutes between the magazine stand and large freezers before Mike MacGrogan could be found. Father

[1] St. John 11: 43, 44.

73

Niemans leafed through *Esquire* and *Time;* he surveyed the contents of the freezers and it occurred to him that the taste of frozen foods was potential only; in their present state there was no difference whatever between corn and blueberries. The manager, when he came, was effusive in his apologies and invited the priest into the back room. "It's not fit for your eyes, Father, but it's private. I'll make us some coffee."

The back room displayed, in lurid colors, naked young women with monstrous breast development, a plastic crucifix, a shimmering picture of the Crucifixion which, if one moved one's head, switched to the Ascension (kneeling figures rose to the air as angels and our Lord sprang up above the clouds), a small American flag and the famous calendar pose of Marilyn Monroe which Father Niemans had seen many times before and his eyes now caressed briefly in acknowledgment. "I'm sorry, Father," said Mike MacGrogan, "I keep telling the boys to clean up back here, but they won't listen. I put that in"—he nodded towards the glittering picture—"to try and influence them, but you can't do anything with young men these days. Protestants," he explained.

Father Niemans nodded and refused the offer of warmed-over coffee. He came directly to the point: John Scudley had been fired; the poor man should be given a job and sympathy; eternal forgiveness was the way of the Lord. "But, Father," protested MacGrogan, "he's done it lots of times, always on company time. I'm a Catholic, Father, but I'm also an American and a businessman. It's not good for business and it's not good for America, this business of killing yourself. He's rejecting the American way of life and if I took him back it would be just as though I'd be supporting a deserter." He grew sad at this, thinking of Molly.

"If your wife would leave you, and go to another man, would you take her back?"

"My wife?" he asked incredulously. This morning her eyes had been so swollen she could hardly see. "Well, yes, I suppose so."

"And if she left you a second time, would you take her back again?"

"I don't know about that. A wife should cleave unto her husband."

"Yes, and the husband, who is stronger, who is her lord, must be always ready to forgive. Would you take her back a second time?"

"I guess so," he answered miserably, blinking at the crucifix until it became a cloud.

"And if she would leave you seven times, you would take her back," Father Niemans declared, not wanting to risk any more questions. "And seven times seven. For so it is written. We must forgive. The Christian man must forgive again and again, as did our Lord"—he pointed Him out—"even to His last breath. Forgive them, for they know not what they do."

"But you can't run a business like that, never knowing if the guy's going to be off killing himself somewhere. I get fresh shipments every day and you got to be able to rely on someone to take care of them."

"Nevertheless," said Father Niemans pompously.

Mike MacGrogan, who felt about priests much as he did about women (he sanctified the thought of them, but their presence made him uncomfortable), was aware of two conflicting desires, both requiring him first to capitulate. He wanted Father Niemans to leave and also wanted to tell him about Molly. "Well, I can't give him back his former job"—he said this to show his independence and to emphasize that, while Christian love and forgiveness had its place, it was not practical—"but maybe I could take him in somewhere else. Delivery boy, that's what he could do. Then if he goes dead on me I can always get a replacement right away."

"Good. I'll leave it to you to inform Mr. Scudley of your decision." Father Niemans congratulated himself; he had done some good, he had added a little piece of dough to the hole in Scudley's soul. He rose.

"Father," MacGrogan said, detaining him, "I have a little problem and, seeing as you're here anyway, I wondered if I could tell you about it."

He sat down again and listened unwillingly to the man's complaints about his young daughter, who had left the house yesterday evening after a "misunderstanding" and hadn't yet returned. He didn't want to call the police, he was a sensible man, he understood these young people, but his wife was getting worried.

"Did you try getting in touch with her friends?" Father Niemans asked.

"Her friends? No, I never thought of that. What would she be doing going to her friends when she can be with her parents? We take good care of that girl, Father, we take too good care of her, I sometimes think. Spoil her, you know. That's how she gets to be so headstrong. Oh, I know, Father, these young people, they're not like we were. A different generation, they have peculiar ideas. But Molly's a good girl at heart, just stubborn as a mule and carries on with all these disreputable elements."

"Oh?"

"All these beatniks, you know, these kids taking dope and I don't know what, all these atheistical youngsters, these Leftists"—he snorted—"all them kids that demonstrate"—his irritation was beginning to blemish his speech—"all them no-good cowards and peaceniks and niggers."

"What?"

"Negroes. She goes around with Negroes. Don't you think that's disgusting, Father?" Seeing the look on Father Niemans' face, he explained: "I'm not against them, no, I'm a reasonable guy. Everybody's got a place, the world's big enough for all of them, but that's no reason why my daughter should be—should be—well, fraternizing."

"Was that the cause of your 'misunderstanding'?"

"What do you mean, Father?"

"Did you disagree about your daughter's companions?"

"Well what do you think, Father? No self-respecting father's going to let his little girl run around with hoodlums and perverts and nig—Negroes."

"I see. I'm afraid, Mr. MacGrogan, I can't help you much. Pray for understanding. Ask our Lady of Guadalupe to intercede for you. Your daughter may come back of her own accord. Pray; and God be with you." The satisfaction he had felt a few minutes before had already evaporated. What kind of message was a priest to bear nowadays? And how deliver it? Head bent, he hurried out of the store and towards the hospital. Fingering his beads, he thought he was nothing more than a caricature of himself.

Mike MacGrogan poured out a cup of coffee, added a shot of whiskey and decided there was no good in anyone any more. Even the priests had been infiltrated.

His daughter was snapping off the head of an unborn crocus. "Johnny," she said happily, "you think my old man's gonna get the fuzz after me?"

"Hope not."

"Silly! It would be a gas, a real gas! They'd never think of looking for me in your pad; they'd have this great big manhunt and never find me. Man! that would be something else, don't you think? You know what I need?"

"What?"

"A pistachio ice-cream cone."

"I guess we can still afford that. O.K."

She stopped him and, with a mature expression attempting to assert itself on her face, asked, "You got money problems? That's bad; we got to do something about that. Hey,

I know! Hey, Johnny, know what we'll do? I just got this great idea! The old bastard doesn't need all his bread. He's got bread, baby, let me tell you, bread all over the house. He's rolling in it and I know where he keeps it."

"Are you suggesting we rob your father?"

"Why not? It'd be a gas and we could get Bix and the other cats to help us. We'd be up to our ears in bread and you could take me to Las Vegas."

"Don't be silly." Of course it was impossible, but still, a charming suggestion. Just compensation. He kissed Molly enthusiastically and picked her up in his arms.

"Hey, crazy, let me down!"

He bought her the pistachio cone (butter pecan for himself) and they strolled through the park until late afternoon. Then they returned home, where Molly spent an hour in the bath with radio, three magazines, nail polish and a bottle of bourbon in a line beside the tub. Her procrastination went unnoticed; Foots came an hour late and she was almost ready by the time he arrived. Scudley handed her over to him with the flourish expected of a thoroughbred owner and, again refusing the invitation to join them, sent them off with friendly greetings to all the cats.

After the door closed, tiredness hit him between the shoulder blades. He turned on the radio and lay down on the floor. A "golden oldie" came on, one of his favorites, and he increased the volume:

> I want a girl
> Just like the girl
> Who married dear old dad. . . .

A twenty-five-year-old smell rose slowly from his chest; a feeling like regret swaddled him and he wanted to rip it off. He picked up the phone and—for the last time, he promised himself—called Mare.

* * *

Marya was well satisfied with her day. It had begun at
ten-thirty, after a dream of being in love with a computer,
feeding herself into it bit by bit until she was entirely con-
sumed. She woke with a package of thought: I could never
be unfaithful to such a husband, except maybe with an
electric toothbrush, and laughed, delighted to be awake and
with herself. Like many people who live alone and are
imaginative, Marya often dreamed with great vividness and
her dreams carried her through morning. For Marya, dreams
could take the place of a companion: a private, secret re-
lationship had developed between her conscious and unconscious minds and the two cohabited with an intimacy
that would seem bizarre or even morbid to anyone who
shares his bed with another person. But Marya, who knew
that being alone is intolerable, sought the company of her
many selves.

She brought coffee and juice to bed, read the first four
chapters of a detective story and then slid luxuriously into
day, first submerging herself in a bubble bath, then spend-
ing almost an hour in preparing herself for lunch. Her
make-up, after half an hour's work, was inconspicuous; her
skin exhaled My Sin under the shocking-pink suit and her
hair style was scrupulously, perfectly uncoiffed.

She drove out to the Tapends' for lunch—he was Chairman of the Department and she, his meek consort—not
dreading as much as usual the "friend" invited for her bene-
fit, the same ineluctable bachelor who, with different names,
ages and professions was someone she "simply must meet"
and who had been "dying to meet her" for the past ten
years. She knew she looked well and behaved accordingly,
to the pride of her hosts. The meal, considering usual gas-
tronomic offerings of the academic community, was excellent, though the wine was a predictable "little thing"—a
Spanish Chablis whose price (only ninety-three cents) was
announced by the Chairman in a voice of self-congratula-

tion. Dr. and Mrs. Wood—a Negro economist and his wife, who taught second grade—and Bill Matcher, a heavy-set sociologist, were the other guests.

Mrs. Tapend shooed them away from Vietnam with little pouts that intimated proximity of tears and small movements of her fingers as though they were ascending a ladder which would lead to armistice of all arguments; her husband opined that "black power" was an unfortunate phrase (Dr. Wood concurred), and, after an interim of university gossip, during which the stupidities of various students were exhibited for general hilarity, they wandered safely through the field of art.

"A friend of mine—you'd be interested by him, Dr. Poum —has just published a novel. A very good one, I think, though he hasn't been accorded the recognition he deserves," said Mr. Matcher. "I'd be very curious to know what you thought of it. My friend feels it's being ignored because his subject matter is taboo in our society."

"It's about romantic love then, is it?"

"Incest, Dr. Poum, and abortion."

"Then I can't understand why it doesn't sell. Is the style too orthodox, perhaps?"

"I have no way of telling, Dr. Poum. I'm not an authority on these matters. I would be very happy if an expert like yourself would read it. The title is *Beside the Blasted Oak*, by William Avery."

William Yeats is laid to rest. Because she had not been able to intercept the look of sourness that now settled on her face, Marya sneezed. "Bless you," said Dr. Wood and his wife echoed, "Bless you."

Later, over coffee, the conversation became more personal. Dr. Wood described his background, a form of Negro lower-middle-class upbringing not uncommon in the South (the others exclaimed their disbelief that he was a Southerner—he showed no trace of it in his accent) and said of

80

his mother, "She was the type of woman whose salivary glands are activated by the sight of a tree. . . ."

He was interrupted by Marya giving a demonstration into her handkerchief. He gave an uncomfortable chuckle and the others were silent. She regretted her impetuosity a moment, then reassured herself and stopped listening. Dr. Wood was light-skinned, wore a Dior tie and was undoubtedly churchgoing. He was unable to talk about himself without seeming to describe a social phenomenon. But she didn't dare interrupt him again.

Nevertheless, it had been a most satisfactory lunch, she thought while driving home at four. The liquor had been abundant, the Tapends had begged her to come soon again —for dinner this time—Bill Matcher had invited her to a concert (she refused) and even the Woods had taken her phone number. As soon as she arrived home, Marya phoned to cancel her date for the evening, preferring the luxury of reading her detective story and getting drunk on her own to a languid dinner with an irreproachable lawyer. When Scudley called, she invited him over.

They spoke about the war ("all balled up," they agreed) and black power ("Makes sense," said Scudley, "just a slogan to get people to buy things, like saying 'Buy American' "). He rested his head in her lap and asked what everything was about. Though she gave no definitive answer, he seemed comforted and rolled over so his face was smothered between her thighs. The heavy smell put him to sleep and Marya, playing with his head, felt peaceful. The evening moved slowly, through words, alcohol and smoke. She didn't mind when he talked baby talk and they didn't make love. When he left, at one in the morning, she felt his absence, if only because the warmth of another creature had been withdrawn from the room. He, shuffling back to the apartment he shared with Molly, was homesick for Mare and felt he loved her as much as the fifty states.

81

*   *   *

Sunday Scudley spent with Molly, Father Niemans with the Lord and Marya with the New York *Times*. Scudley was thinking of his Mare; Marya was thinking of an article she planned to write on Dr. Young[1] for *PMLA*; Molly was lost in entrails and burglaring strategy; and the Lord knew what Father Niemans was thinking.

[1] See p. 120 where Dr. Poum is trying to write the article about Dr. Edward Young (1683–1765) and his long, lugubrious poem *Night Thoughts* (first published 1742, though later added to). This poem rep-represents the English vogue of melancholy, seen in such Gothic works as Thomas Wharton's *Pleasures of Melancholy* (1747) and leading to the Graveyard Poets, best exemplified by Gray's *Elegy* (1750).

8

When he was turned down for the third time that morning, Scudley felt no disappointment. It wasn't as if he'd expected anything. Nothing mattered, so why should it matter if people turned him down? But the job hunt itself, the fact of having to do something about his life, this made Scudley miserable. The whole thing was pointless, a ballpoint pen that wouldn't write any more, but the insight didn't strengthen him. He couldn't bring himself to care what happened, to recognize the importance of making money (he was out looking for a job only because he had told Molly that's what he would be doing) and, as he walked from drugstore to bar, he felt he had no right taking up all this air and space. To be alive, you had to do something— tear apart a goat, whip a girl child—or else there was no sense hanging around. Someone brushed against Scudley and anger exploded in him. He'd like to strangle that guy, castrate him, pull out his entrails like Jack the Ripper and string them on the wall. The spasm passed; Scudley was astonished by it. On his right were the Turkish Baths. Sitting in one of the boxes, melting away little by little, you could turn up the heat, close your eyes and the flesh would become butter, the muscles syrupy, the bones weaving and bending, rubber bones stretching out like taffy. Flesh kneaded into heavy dough, dumped in the Mixmaster, oozing, thinner, spilling from the bowl, the floor covered with pancake dough (little Black Sambo made flapjacks out of tigers), even thinner, so thin the liquid is evaporating, a cloud, a mist, a vapor, poof! "Mr. Scudley, are you all right?"

That handsome priest again, that masqueraded extra who flies in on the tightrope and carries away Tammy Grimes' understudy. "Father, Father—um . . ."

"Niemans." The man had been mortally ill, he told himself to avoid taking offense. A name was a petty thing, after all, a word merely. "I just phoned you but you weren't in."

"What's your problem?"

"My problem? Oh, I see. I only wanted to know how you were. But I can see you're fine now," he said with finality. He had done all he could; no need to prolong the interview.

"I am, eh? Glad to hear it." Stick that beautiful head in horse manure and run a tractor over it. Then fertilize the crops; a priest's always doing good. But, as before, the moment of violence was over immediately and Scudley touched the priest's sleeve with gentleness. "Mind if I walk along with you, Father? I've been looking for jobs all morning and a little break would be fine."

"Didn't Mr. MacGrogan call you?"

"MacGrogan?" How much did this backward-buttoned guy know? Better play dumb. "What's MacGrogan to do with me?"

Either his brain was affected or he was an idiot. "Mr. MacGrogan, at the supermarket. He was going to call you about a job."

"I already talked to him about a job. My job. It's gone."

"But he had another one in mind. I'm sure he'll be in touch with you very soon. He's probably a bit preoccupied right now; he's having a spell of family problems."

"You don't say." Scudley leered.

An idiot, decidedly, but one who didn't seem to believe him. "Yes, his young daughter left home a few days ago."

"His daughter? What d'you think of that! I wonder where she could be."

84

"Probably among friends. I'm sure it's nothing serious but Mr. MacGrogan was a bit disturbed and that's probably the reason he hasn't phoned yet."

"If I were you, I wouldn't hold my breath till he does. People can get drowned that way."

With an effort at courtesy, Father Niemans took his leave from the rude, unpleasant man. Probably paranoiac; so many were these days, the result of television newsreels—or was it free enterprise?—the conviction that someone's out to get you. The devil at work, direct inversion of the feeling that Someone's looking after you. What a nasty man. A good thing, thought Father Niemans, that he never expected gratitude in his profession; otherwise, he might be very annoyed.

"When mild-mannered men try to kill themselves," explained Marya, "they shouldn't be forced back into life."

"I'm not sure I follow," said Father Niemans.

She started to cross her legs, remembered where she was and crossed her ankles instead. She had decided on navy blue for the monastery: it was sober, restrained and yet, unlike black, carried no suggestion of servitude (mourning, and the old Italian women genuflecting in front of their Marias and Francescos with aching, dirty knees and arthritic hands grasping at fat candles).

"I just mean—but who am I to be telling you, Father?" (she didn't pause for an answer)—"that if a shy or gentle man decides to die, he should be respected. That's probably the only decision he's ever made. He's acting on something, he's proving he's a man. Poor Scudley!"

"But it's a sin against the Fifth Commandment. . . ." He wanted to continue, to explain that man can never be master of his own life, but her breasts heaved and quivered as though trying to shake off tiny drops of moisture. "Seven times," she said. "It's vulgar, isn't it? To think that such a lamb would want to die so badly."

"How many times?"

She wet her lips and smiled. "Seven times, my Father."

"The Lord have mercy." He had the strange sensation of Marya growing and spreading, taking up more space, flooding the room. He handed her a catechism and asked her to read the first twenty pages for next time. "We'll talk about it then. And now I thought we'd discuss logical proof for the existence of God." Help my unbelief.

"No, Father, please let's not. Logically, one can prove or disprove His existence through deduction. You come up with an X and can give it any name you please. But I'd like to keep my mind out of religion."

"That's the wrong approach. That's precisely the cause of much unhappiness and intolerance. You see . . ."

"It's very simple, really. Look: if God exists, He must be different from anything else. And since I can believe only in things I've experienced, I have to know Him. I have to feel Him in me and me in Him as St. Theresa did."

"Which St. Theresa?" This was all wrong; the Lord couldn't be approached as a new experience in sensuality; or could He?

"The one in paintings, with her legs spread and the bolts coming down on her."

Father Niemans had nothing to say; a curious impotence, probably requiring confession. He had the feeling Marya was—not frivolous, exactly, but, rather—how to put it?—inconstant of purpose. And yet, there were so many ways of reaching Him. No one could force a particular method, at least not yet. "Eighty-six per cent of Catholics believe Christ is God, but only eighty-one per cent are sure that God exists." What in the world had prompted him to tell her that? It was true—he had read it in last week's *Commonweal* [1]— but really, a most unsuitable fact to bring up on the first day of instruction.

"Marvelous." Her skin pinkened when she laughed and

[1] *Commonweal*, Vol. LXXXII, No. 19.

little lines ran out from her eyes across her temples to her hair. "The Son of God, Who doesn't exist." He's trying to show how liberal he is, she thought, and disapproved.

Her intuition was justified later, when they discussed birth control and war. His remarks were eminently rational, enlightened, humanitarian—and she was disappointed. Here we are, she thought, two young liberals sitting in a monastery, agreeing how things should be. But she comforted herself with his beautiful eyes, his callused knuckles and the knowledge that he had a belovèd in Christ. Nor ever chast, except thou ravish mee. The woman drunken with the blood of saints. She wanted to be swooped up by a lion, carried off on the wings of a dove with seven stars and seven golden candlesticks shedding their light on her. He read from the Psalms before she left and she didn't dare shake hands when she said good-bye. His eyes were intense, his voice low and trembling; with a father like that, she thought, is it incest or blasphemy?

The only rule at Medmenham was that no monk could steal away the nun from another monk. Not many were admitted; only those who were "fair, well-featured and of sweet disposition." [1] Grass pressed down in the forms of lovers, erotic statuary, pornographic literature; the blue bloods of London made their retreat there. Christ's passion is a phrase open to speculation. The nunneries of London were its brothels and the Madame Superiors parceled out their mercy by the hour. What a time to have lived! thought Marya. And yet the Medmenhamites were tame compared with some. The Beggar's Benison carved their motto—"My breath is strange"—on a small silver horn which was blown to lead the novice into an orgy of initiation: autoeroticism,

[1] Jones, *op. cit.* P. 125. The Medmenham Monks were part of the eighteenth-century English tradition of atheistical clubs, the "Hell-fires." They took over the Order of St. Francis at Medmenham Abbey, placed the Thélèmite motto, *Fay ce que Vouldras*, over the doorway and imitated the Rabelaisian order. Sir Francis Dashwood, probably the most famous rake of the time, was Prior, the permanent ruler.

exhibitionism, anal and genital stimulation until climax. Then came suggestive toasts and baptism in the goblet with the strange shape.[1] Too bad it wasn't material for undergraduates. Their dry, constipated little papers on neoclassicism and the influence of Augustine or Lucretius; solemn footnotes on *chinoiserie* (they didn't know the half of it!) and the fashionable tastes of our featured forefathers. Only ten days more. We do our best to revive the old days, she advised the good doctor across two hundred years, Christine Keeler did her part and so did Ward, but it's difficult to mock God these days, He's so hopelessly out of fashion. They've banished Him from Fleet Street to the colonies, where He atrophies, poor dear, through uselessness; though Washington does make use of Him now and again. They've changed His shape a bit, made Him into an eagle—rather charming, don't you know?—reminds one of Jupiter floating about as a swan. And our eagle is every bit as good a rapist as that old bird.

Back at the Triumph. She felt refreshed after dousing herself with acerbity; a necessary douche after that absurd, hot feeling she'd had while he was reading the psalm. The radio went on when she turned the key:

> Don't sit under the apple tree
> With anyone else but me   (oh baby),
> Anyone else but me   (oh baby),
> Anyone else but me.

Even in paradise, a woman wanted the taste of power. Nothing much changes. But when the second-most-famous apple in the world dropped on Sir Isaac's head, it brought us modern gravity. Some fruit.

[1] *Ibid.* P. 185. Jones wrongly attributes "My breath is strange" to the fifth chapter of Leviticus. Actually it is in Job, 19:17. The Beggar's Benison was formed in Scotland and held its initiation ceremonies on St. Andrew's Day (November 30). St. Andrew is Patron Saint of Fishermen and Old Maids and, with St. Columba, Patron Saint of Scotland.

"Man, chick, you're out of your cotton-pickin' mind." Bix had just recently adopted this expression, which he always pronounced with a heavy Southern accent.

"I don't know, Bix. My old man's got all this bread and here we are, this cat he fired and me, his own daughter, and we need it and he's got it. I mean, it's not like taking something away from some poor cat who doesn't have it; I mean, it's not immoral or anything." She curled her legs under her and looked steadily at him with her dilating gray eyes.

"Purr, baby."

"Huh?"

"You're the sweetest little pussy I've seen in a long, long time."

"Bix! The things you say. I'm not, you know I'm not."

"What aincha?"

"That. Pussy."

"Come on, little pussycat, don't have to be shy with old Uncle Bix here. He won't hurt you, he's just an old tomcat and he's prowling for white rats."

She looked at him dubiously. If she had whiskers now, they would be trembling. "You're not being serious."

"Serious? Serious? I want to play cat and mouse with you and you talk of being serious. O.K., kitten, I'll give it to you straight: you want to bust your old man, go ahead and do it. But this old cat's taking no part."

"I can't without you, Bix, you know that. I can't even

drive and Johnny can't hardly and anyway we don't have a car."

"Use a bicycle."

She sighed, about to weep. He rolled another stick for them and she waited in silence until the paper was licked and sealed, the first drag taken and the cigarette placed between her lips. She inhaled and handed it back, "I've never asked you to do anything before and I can't ask Jack any more—you know how he is, and besides, he's got this new chick and with me staying at Johnny's, well it just wouldn't work. It's not like I was asking you to do something *criminal.*"

"Baby, you're something else," said Bix admiringly. She was just a little girl, he thought, who didn't like her daddy—and right she was, the old mother was a bastard—and wanted to get even. But Bix couldn't help her. He'd resolved to go straight twelve years earlier (he was now thirty-five) and had never broken his resolution. Here she sat, this pale little baby with enormous eyes and a body that looked as though it would snap in two with pressure, but there was nothing to be done. He'd been through enough; the risk was too great; he'd be taking twice the chance she would and if you wanted to do the big things you had to save yourself for them, you couldn't afford to help out a little white chick with a grudge against her old man. Even going straight, he'd been locked up and had risked jail dozens of times in the cause. But that was different, that meant something. "No, baby," he said seriously, "I mean it. I'm not your man for this deal."

"Oh"—now she was actually crying and mascara ran in faint streamlets down her cheeks—"Bix, you think I'm a baby, don't you?"

"Sure I do, a sweet little baby. Remember that old song? 'Everybody loves a baby, that's why I'm in love with you, Pretty baby . . .' "

90

"No, stop. Don't you see? Everybody's been treating me that way all my life and it's not fair; I'd like to tear all your insides out. And you, you're supposed to be my best friend and you treat me that way, too. I'll show you all; it would serve you right if I got killed. I'll show you I'm no little kid." She grabbed her pocketbook and stomped out.

"Molly," he called softly.

She turned her head and looked at him with large, sad eyes.

"Come back." He cuddled and comforted her, gave her more pot and put on her favorite old Bessie Smith record. When she recovered, he said that if she was determined to go ahead whether he helped or not, he might just fill her in on a few things, teach her some ground rules and give her what you might call a basic plan. She hugged him tightly, insisted he was her best friend in all the world and she wouldn't ever tear his insides out; she'd do anything for him anytime at all, he'd see. For some reason, her enthusiasm and kittenish affection saddened him; he held her head against his chest and stroked her hair slowly, as though she were a wounded animal that, for its own sake, would have to be gotten rid of.

"Holy Mother of God, not the police, Mickey," pleaded Isla MacGrogan.

"It's four days now, long enough for a fancy spree, and she's under age besides."

"Mickey," begged his wife, whose fear of the police was surpassed only by her fear of the devil, "she's a grown girl. When I was Molly's age we were married—almost." She said the last word in a whisper with fingers crossed, hoping that neither he nor the Lord would hear. She had actually been two months shy of nineteen when they married.

"I don't like them any better than you, lassie," he said, giving her a brief, rough embrace, "but anything might have

91

happened to her, and she's our only one." In this the Mac-Grogans were not so Irish as they seemed, though the fault lay more in heaven than in themselves. Two miscarriages, a stillbirth, another miscarriage and then came Molly, a gift of God bestowed when Isla was twenty-eight. The birth had been difficult and the doctor warned that another might be fatal. MacGrogan and his wife had discussed matters with each other and with a priest and had finally decided not to take a chance. Nowadays, of course, they'd have permission to use the pill, just like any Protestant (and this thought made MacGrogan furious in retrospect); but in 1948 the only method or avenue open to them was ten days monthly of abstinence (Isla had always been somewhat irregular).

His plea to her maternity caused Isla to weep. "My baby. My only baby." She had been taking Communion every morning since Molly's disappearance, and now begged her husband to join her. "Wherever she is, the Lord will have mercy on her poor misguided soul."

"Don't you think, old woman, it's better to get the girl back than pray for her?" Isla nodded dubiously. "I'll give her till tonight. If she's not in her own bed by then, I'm calling the police."

At this, Isla fell to her knees and praised or cajoled the Lord. If He would do nothing for Molly, surely He would do something for her, Isla, His faithful handmaiden who worshiped Him daily. He would protect her from the police. He and His host of angels—led by St. Michael himself—would protect a poor, helpless woman from the terror of the law.

MacGrogan looked at his kneeling wife with a combination of pity and contempt and, after placing his lips a moment on her old, reliable head, left for work. On his drive to the supermarket, he saw a young, broad-shouldered priest on the sidewalk and remembered his promise to Father Niemans. He would call that death-chasing worm as soon as he got in, he vowed. He was a fair man, he stuck by his word and a promise was a promise.

When the phone rang at eight-thirty, Scudley at first didn't hear it. He and Molly had been arguing about the proposed robbery until three in the morning and both were nearing the stage of deepest sleep in their third cycle. Molly, who was closest to the phone, picked it up on its fourth ring. "Mmmm," she said.

"John Scudley?"

"Mmmm." She handed the receiver to him, and he reached across her with closed eyes, one arm under her head, the elbow of the other placed on the far side of her waist. "Yes?"

"John Scudley? This is Mr. MacGrogan."

"What?" Instinctively, he pulled Molly closer. She opened her eyes a crack, saw Scudley silently mouthing the words "your father" and opened them as far as they would go.

"Mr. MacGrogan. Come on, boy, don't play dumb." Though he doesn't have to play it, thought MacGrogan. "I know you were disappointed when I couldn't give you back your job, but it had nothing to do with me. I don't have any grudge against you, I don't have nothing personal, but I've got to think of the customers, see, and of business, you know; you've got to be thinking what's good for business . . ."

"Is good for America," Scudley whispered.

"What's that? Speak up, damn you, can't hear."

"Nothing. Nothing. I was just singing a lullaby my mother taught me."

"Well for crying out loud, can't you behave normal a minute? Leave your lullabies out of this. I got something for you, boy. You'll be pretty surprised to hear this, I don't doubt—by the way, Scudley, never knew you were married."

"I'm not."

93

"But I thought—wasn't that a woman's voice just answered?"

"Oh that—um, that was only—um, my mother. Sort of combination mother-housekeeper. Very good and efficient, got her at the agency that handles . . ."

"Oh shut up." MacGrogan now felt completely justified in having fired Scudley. The pervert not only killed himself; he also kept whores in his house. Still, a promise was a promise, especially when one of those priests was involved. They had ways of making things hot for you. "I have a little surprise for you, boy, a proposition."

"What!" He sat up abruptly, then fell back again on top of Molly, who uttered a little scream before it was squashed by his shoulder blades.

"Yes. I know I seem gruff sometimes, but I'm human, too, you'll be surprised to learn"—he waited for the appreciative chuckle; none came; the worm had no sense of humor; he continued—"and I've decided to give you another chance—you know, forgive and forget. What do you think of working here again?"

"Fine, Mr. MacGrogan."

"Of course you understand I can't give you back your old job—that was a responsible one and, well, let's face it, boy, you just didn't live up to your responsibilities. But I'm willing to give you another chance and I'll take you on as delivery boy. Now, whadya say to that?"

"Thank you, Mr. MacGrogan." He thought how alike their inflections were, Molly's and MacGrogan's. "I can start next Monday."

"Next Monday? I'm offering you a job right now. Are you trying to get smart, young man? Are you making deals with me?"

"No, Mr. MacGrogan, sir."

"Well, then came on down to the store right now."

"I'd rather start Monday, sir." He wasn't the old Scudley; not the guy addicted to fantasies any more; he wasn't

94

just a thing that could be pushed around. There was no reason to wait till Monday; still, Scudley wanted to take advantage of his vacation, now that he knew a job was waiting for him. He could go to the movies, play around with Molly . . . the fact that his body was reclining on the chest of MacGrogan's daughter augmented his courage. He had the winning combination. He could whip old MacGrogan until the guy hopped away screaming, his tail between his legs. The bastard. No reason to take orders from anyone any more. Scudley had his hostage; he could shoot his way out by shooting it up her.

"What do you . . . oh, what's the difference?" he said, surprisingly. "Start Monday. I'm in no mood for arguments."

His courage screwed, as they say, to the bursting point, Scudley contined the conversation. "I understand you've had a bit of trouble lately—something about your daughter, was it?" Molly, her face held in position by Scudley's left arm, stared at him with frightened, delighted eyes.

"How the hell do you know that!"

"Well, sir, just heard from the boys—you're an important man, Mr. MacGrogan, you got to expect that kind of thing. You don't get much privacy with a position like you got."

"Well. I suppose. Yes, the fact is, my little girl's gone off somewhere. Nothing serious but I'm getting the police on it if she's not back by tonight."

"Police?"

Molly giggled and bit Scudley's hand. He didn't cry out, but the hand retreated and Molly began kissing him, rubbing against him. Her tongue found his ear and, like a snake in search of a hole, scurried inside. He tried vainly to push her away. "Are you sure you want to call the police, Mr. MacGrogan?"—she was tickling him—"with the risk of scandal and all? I'm sure your daughter's all right."

"How can you be so damn sure? She's my daughter" —

who was now gently massaging Scudley's testicles with her tongue—"damn it, and I know what to do."

Scudley couldn't bear it any longer. "Yes, sir. See you Monday, sir. Hope you find her." He hung up, slithered away from her mouth and pulled Molly to sitting position. "You've got to go home."

"Why, Johnny? Don't you like me any more?"

"Molly! This is serious. Your old man's calling the cops. Can you think of the mess?"

"A gas." She giggled, slid down and pulled the blankets over her head. Scudley, the eminently reasonable Scudley, argued at length with the bulge, which every now and then let out a muffled "no." But in the end, Molly had to agree. She promised to iron her dress and, since she unconditionally refused to set foot in her parents' house for any reason except to rob it, Scudley made her promise to see her father at the supermarket and thereby forestall the police. To gain this victory, however, Scudley had had to pay with his bit of flesh. Molly had agreed on one condition only: "If I do that, will you promise to help me bust them?"

"Molly . . ."

She could be as pigheaded as her father. "If you don't I won't go down to the store and I'll let the fuzz find me here." Her eyes glittered; she stared straight at him until he dropped his lids and mumbled, "Yes."

"You promise?"

"Yes."

"Swear to it."

"Look, Molly . . ."

"Swear."

He flipped his hands so the palms faced upward and let them sink to the bed.

"Swear."

"What do I swear?"

"That you promise to obey me and do exactly what I say when we bust my father."

96

"O.K."

"No. Say, 'I swear to do what Molly tells me when we bust her father and I'll obey her in everything.'"

"That's too much. I . . . all right." He repeated her sentence.

"Now cross your heart and hope to die."

"I do."

"Say it."

"Cross my heart and hope to die."

"Good. Now come here." Her arms burst open and she was trembling—whether from fear, desire or the attack of new inspiration, Scudley couldn't tell and, after a moment, didn't care.

"The plural allomorph [Z] seems to be learned correctly by a majority of children by the time they reach the age when they enter first grade, at five and a half or six. . . ." Why, thought Marya angrily, couldn't the dumb girl say that most six-year-olds form correct plurals, and have done with it? All these brats would need four years after the B.A. to unlearn the jargon that was eating up their brains. If they ever would. She pushed aside the papers from Freshman English and turned to those from her seminar. "Although *Das Kapital* exerted negligible influence on the literary works of Marxist authors, it would be too hasty to assume that the seminal nature of . . ." Another case of it. Gobbledygook would soon take over the world. It was virulent, highly infectious and took many forms. Academic gobbledygook was probably the most benign. Newspeak, commercials, magazine ads, the language of fashion magazines, television, disc jockeys . . . and in the end, she thought grimly, we'll all suffocate under mountains of diarrhea thrown up from the mouth. "Communist menace from the north," "escalation"—language-wise, we are doomed to end as we began, in a sea of babble. In academia, a sea of "quintessences"—"The quintessential arcaneness of the multifaceted protagonist," one student had written—for which the only palliative was the natural disease of common platitudes. In politics, a more dangerous malady. The peace-loving nations of the free world, attempting to make it safe for democracy, would, in their finest hour, blast their loving, peaceful world to binary digits (bits); and in the holocaust a slow, drawling voice would be heard proclaiming, "Fight for peace; God is on our side."

She needed the comfort of the eighteenth century. Wit was the only assurance—a fine veneer of careful phrasing which protected the tastes of aristocratic minds and plugged up the chinks in society. Ah, finally a student with charity (or laziness) who began his paper with a long quotation from Pope's Second Epistle:

> But what are these to great Atossa's mind?
> Scarce once herself, by turns all Womankind! . . .
> Who breaks with her, provokes Revenge from Hell,
> But he's a bolder man who dares be well.
> Her every turn with Violence pursued,
> Nor more a storm her Hate than Gratitude:
> To that each Passion turns, or soon or late;
> Love, if it makes her yield, must make her hate:
> Superiors? death! and Equals? what a curse!
> But an Inferior not dependent? worse.
> Offend her, and she knows not to forgive;
> Oblige her, and she'll hate you while you live:
> But die, and she'll adore you—Then the Bust
> And Temple rise—then fall again to dust. . . .

She looked for the author of this splendid transcription; whatever he might say in his paper, he was assured of an A. Buff Willis—the young man who had comforted Marya last week when the hospital phoned. What a sweet boy, she thought—blond crew cut, hazel eyes—and became suspicious. Had he chosen this poem as a way of testing her? Or, worse, to indicate that he understood the type of woman she was? At least he had chosen Atossa and not that hateful Chloe ("Virtue she finds too painful an endeavor/Content to dwell in Decencies for ever"). The phone rang and, with the circumstantial inevitability that seems contrived or implausible in novels and is hardly noticed when it occurs in life, it was Buff Willis, asking her to go to the theater with him—*after* the term was over, of course. "I know it's against university policy for students and faculty to fraternize, but I won't be a student any more after next Wednesday." She remembered he was a senior; she said she would think about it. He was tall and strongly built, seemed older than—what was he? My God! no more than twenty-one. "What will you do after graduation, Buff?"

"Bum around Europe a while, I guess, then go into my father's business—steel."

The word thrilled her. "What about the draft? Aren't you afraid they'll call you up?"

"Hell, no. Anytime they want me I'm ready."

She smiled. They'd never call up a young man who worked in steel. Indispensable to the nation's economy, engaged in the war effort, helping to forge all our indispensable deaths. Even after the blast, he and his 2.4 children would be reading the Dow-Jones index in a suburb of heaven. She liked his drawl and remembered the clearness of his eyes, his height. "You're from the Southwest, aren't you?"

"Texas. I thought you couldn't tell any more. Thought I'd become like the rest of you Yanks." His voice played with her; she noticed she was fondling her right breast.

"Thanks for the invitation, Buff. I'll let you know *after* the exam."

They both laughed. Really, his affinity for Pope was admirable and his work had been consistently good. He would go far, perhaps even to the presidency of U.S. Steel. It might be worth while for her to scratch him while she could

99

—a little scar which could be picked in some unfriendly future. What nonsense, she told herself, and imagined the Joint Chiefs of Staff coming through the door, tongues hanging out, panting. Behind them, the Foreign Heads of State were striding and saluting, crying: *"La gloire n'est pas encore arrivée. Mssrs., donnez-nous la gloire. Nous présiderons sur tous. Liberté, égalité, maternité!"* She hung up; the Joint Chiefs of Staff got down on their knees and flapped their ears. The Foreign Heads of State were still shouting: *"Marie Antoinette. Nous avons besoin d'une Marie. Avec nous, le déluge. Nous sommes de l'empire, de Gaul. Dieu est notre droit. Commençons le marché en commun. Vive la . . ."* She couldn't think of the word in French and gave herself over to be licked.

❀ ❀ 10

They arrived at 7:45 and the door was opened by a belching Scudley. Molly, in the next room, was tearing around like a toy beetle with remote control, her feelers in the air, the stripes of her T-shirt much too bright. Every time she hit the wall or an object, her mechanism made her back away precipitately and race off in the other direction.

"Whoa!"

"Bix! You came! You came after all. I love you, ooh how I love you! Hi, Foots, Jo-jo."

"Hi," they answered in unison and twiddled their thumbs. Bix explained that he still did not approve, that he didn't intend to get mixed up in all this, that they could split the money four ways and leave him out; but he was along for the ride and, since he'd masterminded it, he thought he'd wait in the car just to see how things went. Molly attempted to climb up him in her enthusiasm, but he brushed her off. Scudley, whose face had turned a dull shade of green and whose belches were now beginning to be accompanied by other, less acceptable sounds and smells, offered coffee. "No, thank you," answered Foots and Jo-jo, again in unison, suggesting that their research for this adventure had been *Through the Looking Glass*. Bix spat into the ashtray and Molly said, "I guess no one wants any. That was nice of you though, Johnny. Are you all right?"

As though following some previously given stage directions, Scudley's reply was to grab the seat of his trousers with both hands and gallop off in the direction of the bathroom. Molly smiled peacefully. "He's not used to this kind of thing," she explained.

"Mmff," replied the two and placed their hands on their stomachs.

Now Bix took over, lined up the four "yellow-bellied knickknacks," as he called them and manfully spat out instructions. "First of all, I want you to keep a tight asshole. Just remember that, all of you. Stop giggling, Foots, a closed mouth, too. Tight asshole, closed mouth . . ."

"He's like a disease," said Jo-jo. "Foots and mouth disease."

"You can't have your foot in your mouth and eat it, too," elaborated Scudley, feeling giddy.

"What's afoots?" asked Molly and Bix blew up.

"Can't any of you cats stop your pussyfooting around? For Christ's sake, you washouts, whadya think this is?"

"A cat house." Scudley didn't mean to be insolent; his brain was churned up as it had been at the laundromat and he couldn't duck the inspiration when it hit.

Bix glowered at him. "Don't know why I got mixed up with you losers. Come on, now, look smart or we'll all get screwed."

"In the tight asshole." Scudley couldn't resist and was banished to the bathroom for the duration.

The plans had been made days ago; Bix now simply repeated them and brought out the map of the house he had made according to Molly's description. Foots would be at the wheel of Bix's old Dodge, with Bix in back, hidden under blankets. Operation Bust would begin promptly at 8:50, after MacGrogan had left for work and his wife was still sleeping. Then they would enter the house, which, as Molly described it, was simple and functional, a fact not immediately noticed in the distraction of chintz, flowered carpets, our Saviour, bric-a-brac, furniture as respectable

102

and lurid as the crimson lips of withered women in church on Sunday and, of course, crucifixes. Downstairs, a large living room, smaller dining room and next to it the combination kitchen-breakfast nook from which one could step out on a small porch to take one's orange juice and vitamin pills in the sun. Upstairs, two bedrooms, each with connecting bathroom (Molly's was tiny; she could wash her hands while sitting on the toilet), and a spare room, appropriated, when the television was moved into the master bedroom, by Isla for her sewing and, as she called them, "chores." In this room, under a pile of material bought in sales too provocative to resist (most of the fabrics were flowered prints), lay five hundred-dollar bills, a replica of the MacGrogan's original "nest egg," now resting cozily beneath the effusion of bloom, presumably in hopes that it would hatch. In the room where MacGrogan and his wife lay parallel in twin beds, another two hundred dollars were kept behind the portrait of a stern, buxom woman who had been Molly's great-aunt, distinguished for housing, feeding and protecting twenty young men from the I.R.A. and for preserving her virginity until two days before her death.

Each was to follow a separate route, indicated on the diagram by different colored pencils, and Molly could pilfer the nest egg by herself. Now that he had finished reviewing the plan of action, Bix summoned back Scudley from exile, and he came in on all fours, mooing gently and offering free milk to anyone who would come and suck. Molly immediately dropped to her knees beside him and Bix, not sure whether her mouth was opening for prayer or something else, jumped on top of her. She rolled back and he, expecting more resistance, crashed into the legs of the table, from which breakfast dishes splattered in all directions, the cream, appropriately, dripping from Scudley's hair. Jo-jo and Foots tittered from their dry, safe distance and Molly looked puzzled. "What you do that for, Bix?"

103

In answer, from the apartment above, a hammer started pounding the floor and dishes crashed. She smiled happily. "They want to play with us. Let's throw some dishes on the ceiling." Jo-jo and Foots began to yodel upwards and Scudley got to his feet to howl.

As usual, Bix restored order by simply reminding them that if they didn't leave this minute Operation Bust could never be pulled off. He despised all this monkeying around, picked pieces of china out of Molly's hair and hustled them out.

When they got to the car, they found a policeman standing next to it. "This yours?" he asked Scudley.

"No. Why?"

"My mother has a car like this," he said wistfully. "It's illegally parked, too close to the hydrant. My mother does the same thing, always parks too close to a hydrant. A peculiar thing, that. I must of told her a million times. 'Ma,' I say, 'keep your distance. Don't get too close to them hydrants.' But she takes no heed and she's got a whole stack of green tickets at home. Keeps them in the cookie jar. Wonder what it is about this type car. Must be something psychological."

"I'll move it, officer," said Bix.

"It's yours?"

"Yeah, it's mine. Send your mother my love."

"Will do."

"Nuts," declared Bix as they drove away. "Out of his tiny little peanut mind." At the second corner he stopped so Foots could take over the wheel.

"I thought he was cute," said Molly.

They arrived at the MacGrogan house two minutes ahead of schedule and entered, nevertheless, from the rear. Molly walked in straight and purposefully, Scudley followed her with eyes closed and the other two crouched as near to the ground as possible. The four cats prowled the house, each

104

in his own bag. The gray-green hump of a dwarf rose from the pantry; Scudley saw the hump, hard as metal, filled with viscousness, a cunning hump that kept him transfixed in the center of the kitchen until he was pushed forward by the heads of Jo-jo and Foots. By the grace of God and lesser-known powers, Scudley didn't scream, cough or even speak. He went dead white, then streaks of green fluttered across his face from his ears to his nose, but he couldn't speak. Jo-jo and Foots, their crania pressing on Scudley's buttocks, uttered muffled groans and Molly, at the head of the procession, sneezed. It was for sure, Scudley knew, that all the devils had been released. A long snake slithered across the hall, wound itself into the rug and pinwheels of flowers burst from its scales. From above, where the lighting fixtures hung, disembodied hands and feet waved at him. Sweat ran down his forehead, into his eyes and he was still being propelled forward by the thick skulls of both men. Molly stopped and he crashed into her. Jo-jo and Foots fell to the floor (but made little sound, since they had been so close to it all along) and Molly, the sole biped now, examined the scene with distaste. Her fellow conspirators were sprawled around her; Jo-jo and Foots looked up sheepishly, with fat, bland twin smiles. Scudley was rolled into a ball; his eyes were closed, his skin white and he said nothing. Silently, she gathered them up one by one, made sure they could remain on their feet without falling, lined them up with nine inches between each and led them up the stairway like a mountain guide, having first attached the party to a rope and now taking them up the most precipitous part of the rock.

At the top she released them, sent the two grinning cats on reconnaissance, indicated, with a tilt of her chin, that Scudley was to invade her mother's bedroom, and then went off in the direction of the sewing room. Scudley, his knees tight together as though suffering from cold or locked

105

in a paroxysm of prayer, used both hands to push himself along. As he moved, the jungle animals flashed neon eyes and stuck out glittering tongues. A sloth, hanging upside down in the doorway, nipped his nose. A mountain elephant picked up a hydra and snorted. In the wings rested two mermaids, their hair dripping, coral oozing from their navels, their faces black and stuck everywhere with spikes. The tails of tigers rippled through the air, too fast to see, and in the far corner of the half-lighted bedroom waited a satyr, pawing impatiently, to trample poor Scudley when he entered. Scudley threw his arms straight out and pulled himself forward. He could still move, and bravely he came into the room as though none of the thousand horrors lurked there. The satyr turned Pegasus, took off and whizzed past Scudley's head. Scudley dropped to his knees. Jo-jo peered in, came up to Scudley and delivered a stream of sound like an enormous tapeworm into his ear. Scudley fell forward and lay prone. He felt hands, claws, tentacles pick him up and then he was on his feet again, all alone. But not really, he saw with horror. Something was moving on the bed, something huge and lumpy and pink. The dwarf again, his hump disguised under bedclothes. But Scudley was now resolute; dwarfs, demons, ghoulies, ghosties and wee beasties could no longer deter him; nor the thing on the bed that went bump in the night. Erect and fearless, Scudley approached the picture, took hold of one corner, lifted it, felt underneath for the money, felt something soft and squooshy, the texture of mucous or jellyfish, and his hand shot away again; the picture tilted, Molly's great-aunt squinted a curse at him and crashed down in an avalanche of glass. Scudley brought a fist above his head, pounded himself down to the ground, then gave himself a kick till he rolled under the bed. Underneath, he felt the bed moan as its occupant burst into consciousness, sat up, gave the air a sound thrashing, and yelped.

106

She was terrified, much too frightened to get up and see what was the matter, so she rocked on her bed, moaned, and implored the saints to go investigate. Then she felt easier. Her deputies sent ahead, Isla MacGrogan now dared to peel off the covers cautiously and open her eyes. She squinted around the room and the bed sagged towards Scudley's right ribs. She got up; the bed shook itself free of her memory and, sighing, straightened out. Underneath, Scudley echoed the sigh (but silently) and, without moving his head, observed feet clad in gauze rosebuds shuffle over the blossoming carpet and out of the room. He sighed again and turned over.

Molly, hearing the crash, had dived into the pile of flowered prints and now lay trembling in her nest, not knowing whether her fear was of the police, asphyxiation or of her mother, who would immediately begin to pray. Jo-jo raced into the hall, where to his complete terror he was crashed into by murderer or maniac. The maniac, just as terrified, tried to bury his face in the carpet and remained there while Jo-jo recognized him as Foots, kicked him sharply and ran down the stairs. Still Foots remained, his jackknife position no longer so angular, until Isla MacGrogan stubbed her rosebuds on him. She looked down to see the offending obstacle. "Are you a person?" she inquired.

"Uhhh," he muttered into the flowers.

"A man?"

His reply was the same as before.

"Then what are you doing on my carpet like that?"

He cocked his head and squinted up at her. "I'm frightened."

"No need to be. I was frightened, too, glory knows, when I heard that noise. But it's all right now, I saw what it was, just Great-aunt Molly on the floor. Poor dear"—she sighed —"she'd positively loathe such treatment and there she is, like any common hussy, lying on the bedroom floor with all that glass around her. But don't you worry, young man, I'll get her up and righted good as new. And a new pane."

"Pain?" Foots moved and caused his own downfall. Sitting now more or less as men are meant to sit, though with legs sprawled, he contemplated his interlocutress while she contemplated him. "Pain in the ass," she said and startled him.

"Pain in the ass?"

"Yes, of course; if this one broke, we'll just have to get another. Not too expensive, I don't think. I'll send you to jail," she added and her eyes beamed.

"No, don't."

"No need to be upset. It's not because of your color. I often think of turds. I like them, you see, I speak to them."

"Turds?"

"What? Can't hear too well; I'm a bit deaf, don't you know."

"Did you say you speak to turds?" he shouted.

"Oh, yes, I can hear you well. Not all of them, only the little ones. Those that have flecks of yellow are my favorites. Don't you feel well? It's rude to make that sound, you know. And those with the large red spots . . . You *do* seem to be ill. Can I get you something? I know a marvelous brew, urine and money, sometimes with a dash of scum. Would you like to try?"

"Glg." He rolled over and lay flat.

"Well, then. Oh, by the way, young man, I've been meaning to ask you something. Do roll over so I can cook you."

Adamantly, he held his ground and Isla, a bit put out by his manners, recognized that he was a Negro and therefore persecuted and so probably suspicious of all white people, even one so well meaning as she. The Lord had made them all, in His infinite wisdom and understanding. "I meant to ask you what you were doing here. Did you want to see me? Did you want to smell me something? I'm sorry, but I can't

108

really use anything more. I have all the lushes I need, all the nine fucks and coons, all the plates and bowels. So you see? I'm very well shocked."

"Glad to hear it. Where's the gore?"

"The door? Well, you must have seen it coming in, mustn't you? Still, you seem shit so I'll bake you." She bent to help him up, then guided him down the stairs and out the door. Coming up again, she wondered about the younger generation and shook her head. Such evidences of rude behavior and ill-health made her think of Molly and she worried about her daughter. This new generation coming up was very peculiar, no one could understand them any more, they didn't even speak English and they seemed to take no care whatever of their health. Skipping meals and getting too little sleep—that was probably the cause of it. This young Negro fellow was too ill to move. He should have accepted the lemon and honey, but then, they're all so independent they don't accept help from anyone. She shrugged her shoulders, wrapped her robe closer and went to wash her face. The saints, she reminded herself, had worse trials to undergo, but none of them, as far as she could remember, ever had to deal with a Negro.

Molly, having heard sounds from the hall, remained covered and tried to calm herself by thinking of the ages of all movie stars whose last names begin with a P. Peck and Presley were easy because you'd heard them so often, but there were no others she could think of, not Price or Pert or Prince or Pannapristie. Then footsteps moved down the stairs—two people it seemed—then up again, only one, and now silence. She hadn't found the money; it must have been removed or "borrowed" by her father—he sometimes did that, the bastard—she didn't care. She waited another few minutes and prayed: Paul and Ringo, Let me swing—O George and John, Put me on. Then she burst out, flowers fluttering and falling around her, ran out the door, down the

109

stairs and made it to the street, where the Dodge was just getting ready to pull away. Jo-jo and Foots were inside; they opened a door and hauled in Molly. "Dough?" "No." "No bread?" "That's what I said, man." "What a mother!" "Yeah. Where's Johnny?" "Dunno." "No? What you do with him?" "Nothing." "Nothing? Well, that's a bitch. What do we do now?" "Nothing. C'mon. There's no way of getting that cat out of the bag he's in." "Guess you're right, Bix." "Yeah. So this whole bust was what you'd call a fiasco, right?" "Bix, don't say that; it just didn't make it." "You telling me something, baby?" He pressed hard on the accelerator and raced the car back to his place. No one said another word.

Scudley, too, was silent. Under the bed, he dozed a while (and had heard none of the exchange in the hall) and woke to see rosebud slippers padding towards him. For a moment, he thought he must be dead and in heaven, where small pink clouds scurried over the thick blue pile of the sky. But he realized, when the clouds were thrown off to reveal gnarled, knobby feet, that he had failed again. No sweet death, this; more like a Cistercian in his coffin, whiling away the time before the grave *in memento mori*. The feet were very close, almost touching him. An article of clothing, something lacy and pink, fell on one side of them. Would an arm, with perhaps a body attached, swoop down to claim it? Scudley screwed tight his eyes, and when he pried them open later, the pink fluff had disappeared. He was dreaming, he told himself, and to confirm it shut his eyes again.

He slept comfortably, considering the austere nature of his mattress, for two hours, after which he woke himself by yawning loudly. Isla had meanwhile bathed and dressed, made breakfast and the bed (a simple process of patting back whatever had come up during the night, then covering the whole thing with rosy-fingered down), swept up the offending particles around Aunt Molly and gone out to do the shopping. So when Scudley woke, he saw nothing but the floor with its covering of blue stretching on both sides of him, heard nothing but sounds of day and traffic from outside the house, sat up, banged his head sharply, fell back again. Then he pondered his predicament, the condition of being mortal, the sad flight of women. When his head stopped throwing out sparks, he rolled out from under the bed, stood up, dusted himself off and went to the bathroom. He washed his face and hands, saw that he had forgotten to shave this morning but, finding only an electric razor in the MacGrogan's cabinet, decided to forgo that part of his toilet for the day. Nevertheless, he splashed on some after-shave lotion (though he picked the wrong bottle and afterwards regretted his aroma of roses) and went downstairs, where, to his satisfaction, he saw that breakfast was laid. The dishes were dirty, true, and the jam sticky and the toast cold, but still, it was nice to find breakfast waiting after you'd been through such a confusing morning. He sat down and began to eat. Halfway through his toast, he was interrupted by the arrival of Isla MacGrogan, who came through the kitchen laden with groceries. Scudley jumped up and helped her; she thanked him; he nodded and went out through the door she had left open.

When he hadn't returned by noon (they were phoning his apartment every fifteen minutes in case he had gone there), his friends grew worried. At three, they decided the worst had happened, he'd been caught and thrown inside. Though they knew he wouldn't spill—you could count on old Johnny Scudley—they didn't see any means of rescuing him or even of discovering where he was. They couldn't very well go over to the Place and ask if he was registered, Molly pointed out and, though anxious to help, they recognized the futility of prowling around; there was nothing they wouldn't do for old Johnny, they assured each other, but

111

there was nothing they could do either. Having cleared themselves by confessing their intentions, the cats at Bix's rolled their own and, between giggling and dozing, let the day go to pot.

Scudley passed the day aimlessly, window-shopping, walking through the park, playing ball with some skinny kids, then walking along again—a church on the right—going inside and reading out of the psalter for a few minutes. This morning, with all the excitement and inspiration and the pale-green feeling that invaded his body, Scudley had forgotten to take his wallet and now, penniless, he was denied all fruits of his society—the movies, Turkish baths, taxi rides and—most important—food. He thought of going home but Molly and maybe even the others might be there and he couldn't face them yet. He thought of going to Mac-Grogan and asking for a few bucks, but decided it somehow wasn't right, just in case the old lady had said something. Besides, being hungry had an advantage: though Scudley meant to be thinking nothing, feeling nothing, still, every now and then an image, a setting, the beginnings of a little scene would pop up in his mind like toast that's ready and he'd have to get rid of it quickly before the word "fantasy," fanning out like a peacock's tail, could unfurl above the image and bring along goats, welts and the body of a dead child being violated. He could remember his hunger and concentrate on that; if the germs of images became virulent, they could spread into steaks, shortcakes and avocado pears. If he could be hungry enough never to summon up those pictures, he might yet be saved. He felt nostalgic: so much of his time had been spent dreaming and he really loved his old dreams of slipping away under the snow, the sea, being propelled to the stars, but now they'd been tampered with and ever since Bix had shown him the "fantasies," Scudley couldn't return to his simple, peaceful pleasures of death. His imagination, once so predictable and satisfying, was now

112

ravaged by sexual violence and he didn't dare any more to let in one dream or one image, for fear it would go the way of those others. Hunger was a good ploy; if he could be hungry enough, his fantasies wouldn't betray him with sex but would offer food instead. So he didn't go to MacGrogan, didn't see if he could get a hamburger on credit at the diner and firmly dismissed the idea of calling Mare.

He concentrated on hunger and by five his imaginings were all of meat. Thick chops, pork tenderloin, strips of bacon, a sea of calves liver oozing around him like jellyfish. By 5:20 the meat was becoming rancid and he quickly put all the pieces in the freezer. At 5:25 he found himself in front of the supermarket. He gazed in reverence, realizing only now how much he had missed it, how futile his life had been during the past ten days. Too much had been happening; the tumult of events, people, emotions had wrung him like a spin-dryer and he had almost forgotten the simplicity and peace of his former life. With the memory of his days here, filling carts, stacking boxes, dreaming, stamping prices on containers, came also the memory of lying with his head between Mare's breasts; and another memory, very indistinct, of something like a meadow, where flowers or tall grasses covered him completely. Everything had to be made silent again; a life of crime, drugs and women was not for him. He moved closer, intending nothing; the invisible eye caught sight of him and rolled apart the doors. He entered, where the air smelled hard and of nothing natural, where the bright display of colors, shapes, typography all blended smoothly as pablum, where the canned Muzak spilled its benediction over unheeding customers (they also serve who buy) and tides of culture (something like Beethoven, he guessed, or the "New World" Symphony) washed away the cares of the day. A baptism of shapes and sound, an indistinguishable lullaby which comforted Scudley (an Aquarian) for being born in a country plagued by freedom of

113

choice. No one noticed him; his former co-workers all were engrossed in closing up for the night. Scudley was content. Here, in the promised land, decisions could be made without consequences ("Money back in 10 days if not entirely satisfied") and the grasping hand moving down the aisles found its object with no more difficulty than the mouth of a nursing infant.

Scudley thought of his parents—his mother, really, since the memory of his father had faded away like an old soldier into some Retirement City, where age, sex and personality no longer exist and only the prepaid tombstone identifies the customer. His father had, in fact, been a military man, of large physique but low rank and small fortune. He had died when Scudley was eight and all that remained of him were pale eyes and an arm outstretched to the horizon. Mrs. Scudley, who died five years ago, had been an affectionate and rigid mother, protecting Scudley from harm while holding up to him examples of moral stature. She chose men who were temperate and humorless, hated sin and injustice and had made their lives into models of complaisant verbosity. Though Mrs. Scudley was very busy in the community, mending souls, preparing jams and tonics, she often found time for her children. Johnny and his sister, Susan (now married to an insurance broker and living in Hartford, from where she sent Christmas cards and counsel), spent a happy childhood of balanced diets, fresh air and exercise, occasional trips to the mountains and Sunday school. They had been taught early that life had a bland flavor, and by the time he was ten, Johnny possessed the precocious knowledge that happiness lay in contented monotony. The lessons of childhood never left him and even now, when Scudley was forced to taste a raw slice of life, he choked and couldn't bring it down.

He thought of his kindly, balding mother as he walked past the meat compartment and realized that the past ten

114

days must have seen her turn over in her grave so often that she was probably bruised and arthritic. A good thing she had died before she could see her only son fraternize with thieves and pornographers. He picked up a slab of steak, beautifully marbled with fat, hard and glistening under its cellophane cover. He walked farther back and came to the door of the freezer. He opened and entered. It was five-thirty now, the last customers were lined up for the only cashier and the fresh fruits and vegetables were covered for the night. He thought of Mare as he walked towards the cold and wished she were with him. How glorious it would be, to suffocate between her thighs. What a lovely lady. He offered up a prayer to her, begging her to think of him kindly, to remember that her lips had once held him tightly; and he prayed that mercy would be shown in her remembrance of him. When he was gone, she would think that he'd performed the act of a real man; and by dying, he would erect himself in her mind.

The lights were going out. The employees in the meat department had gone home already. Scudley found a wooden box, stood on it, reached behind to bunch up the material of his shirt and successfully harpooned the cloth on a meat hook. He kicked away the box, folded his arms across his abdomen, bent his neck and, hung between two sides of beef, waited to be frozen into eternity.

After ten minutes he sneezed five times and could feel the material rip. But it still held him and he dared not reach back to investigate the damage. He swung gently from the meat hook in hopes it would not reject him. He was very cold, but still too conscious of the sensation of cold. And then, his feet disappeared. Joyfully, he realized that he felt nothing in them at all, not cold, heat or pain. Carefully, he rubbed one foot against the other; happiness gurgled in him when he recognized that they were completely numb. Now his hands—they, too, were becoming

115

nothing, insensate objects at the extremities of limbs. Soon, soon, it would happen: he opened his eyes wide so the tears of pleasure could freeze. His soon-to-be-frozen heart pumped its gratitude and Scudley was stroked by icy fingers of bliss. Kelvin was his god and he would descend lower than anything had ever done, coming closer to perfection than even the Russians. Soon, very soon now, his body would be hard as steak and not the fires of hell could thaw him. In perfect preservation, Scudley would exist forever, a man firmer and harder than all others, a man who had the heroism to turn himself into an object (perfect, imperishable) and who was therefore the ideal emblem of his country's strength.

At ten minutes to six the shirt tore through and Scudley fell. To his anguish, he discovered he could walk almost normally and he groped in the dark room, rubbing himself for warmth, until he found the door. Both exits of the supermarket were already locked and Scudley let himself out through a window like a fugitive who has been ejected once again from a country where he sought asylum.

▶▶ 11

"Even you," she said, "even you must have an anthropomorphic image of God from time to time. It can't be blasphemy; visions get trained the way our eyes do. We see only what's familiar." She was with him for the second time this week (it was Friday) because the last faculty meeting of the year would be held Monday afternoon and she couldn't afford to miss it.

"To see human representations of God is not the same as seeing Him. Wait for . . ." How could he talk to her, when her skin bore angry flushes and her eyes seemed infected by fever?

" 'Like one who sees in a dream and afterwards the passion of the dream remains though the rest is lost, such a one am I.' *Paradiso*, I think." Last night the priest, wearing a purple cassock in front of Grauman's Chinese Theatre, made her kneel in front of him and remove her underwear. He bent down and massaged her clitoris with his fingers. Children were crying; he caught her hair in his hand, chopped it off and threw her back. She had a child in her arms, a little girl who toyed with her breasts and was naked under the frilly pinafore. Then the child was gone; Marya and the priest walked into the theater-temple and lay down in a large meadow of deep-blue cornflowers and black-eyed Susans, though the smell was of honeysuckle. He was naked to the waist; she tore off her blouse and her arms reached up, pulled him down by the neck so he was lying on her

117

with his full weight and their nipples met. Her eyes were closed, her lips blindly searched for his. "Not yet," he said, extricating himself gently and when she woke she was extremely happy. "Not yet" meant that someday—and it would be soon—he'd take her to him, he'd claim her. A sentence floated up to consciousness: "The female in me loves God through my priest, but the male in me loves Him directly, a spear aimed at His Word." Last night, she'd come so close to divinity she almost came. "I had a dream about you . . . no, never mind."

He cocked his head and wondered what, in the name of all that's good and holy, she was thinking. "Did you have time to go over any of the catechism?"

"That. Father, listen. I can't tell you . . . some sort of violence . . . I'm not rational." The good doctor knew it; imagination is dangerous to reason. On the other hand, this was another country, a different time and the sabotage of polished phrases might be justified in an Age of Unreason.

"Did you read the paper today?" he asked, just to calm her down and relieve the dazzle in her eyes. She frightened him with her breathless intensity. Ten days ago he'd met a wry, skeptical professor of English and now he had a candidate for beatitude on his hands. He didn't know quite what to make of it. Was this heresy or mysticism? In either case, he preferred to avoid it. Father Stephen had remarked this morning that the lady who came to visit looked like the heroine of a movie he'd recently seen; and he'd answered smilingly that she was a professor (but the pride he felt!), avoiding the eyes of the good old monk, who might read through them to the soul of Father Niemans, a soul ready to place itself in danger, to take on the temptations of St. Anthony with the gusto of a prize fighter about to challenge the champion. His soul, Father Niemans knew, was playing with hell-fire. But now she was tempting him with a passion which might, for all he knew, be the reverse of Satanic. The

118

devil was often known to take a woman's shape, but how often had that form housed our Lord? (Carnal reveries didn't count.) St. Theresa, St. Catherine—that strange, emaciated woman who in the end could take no nourishment except the Eucharist, who slept only half an hour every two days, deposed the Pope at Avignon, organized the last Crusade, had male secretaries and held a decapitated head in her hands. The Lord had taught her to read; she prayed that He take her heart and replace it with His, which, according to the testimony of the Blessèd Raymond, He did after an interval of a few days when Catherine of Siena lived without a heart.[1] Women, even the saints, were strange. Their urgency, the passion in them, went quite beyond his understanding. Perhaps it had something to do with biology. "These gangs of young boys attacking people for no reason. I find it very disturbing. You see such stories almost every day. What do you think it is our young people are lacking?" Current events were much safer than supernatural ones.

He had succeeded; her eyes grew duller and she collected herself as after flight. The ecstatic phrases were whisked out and replaced by rational sentences. (Words from the letters of St. Catherine had been circling around her: "I will, then, that you lock you in the open side of the Son of God, which is an open treasure-house, full of fragrance, even so that sin itself there becomes fragrant. There rests the sweet Bride on the bed of fire and blood."[2] She couldn't know that their thoughts had dovetailed; that the community of men, or thoughts, is potent enough to allow belief in the community of saints. To her, Catherine exemplified the only kind of religion she could temperamentally understand: the fire- and sperm-eating type.) "It's nothing new, this killing

[1] Maynard, Theodore, *Saints for Our Times.* Image Books (Doubleday & Co.). Garden City, New York, 1955. P. 66.
[2] From *Letters of St. Catherine*, a letter to the Blessèd Raymond of Capua on the occasion of the beheading of Niccolò Tuldo.

for kicks, just better organized these days and more widely publicized." The Mohocks took to the streets at night, attacking anyone they saw, raping women and putting out the eyes of old men (a sport called "tipping the lion upon them"). In taverns, they would break glass or furniture; one story told of them throwing linens, chairs, cutlery and whatever else they could get hold of out the second-story window. When the landlady protested, they threw her out after her possessions, and when informed of her demise, they laughed and told the innkeeper (her husband) to add her to the bill.[1] But the Mohocks were blue bloods, sons of noblemen, and not much could be done to stop them. Today crime was more democratic; time overflowed even from the hands of the working class and everyone could be careless with life, property and the pursuit of happiness. "Though I do think it's true that hate is on the increase. Still, a practical method for controlling overpopulation."

She was peculiar, no doubt about it. These pendulum swings of hers, this morbidity in her that would lash out like a whip, the strange rapt mood that would come over her— all these made him dizzy and uncomfortable. He decided to read her a psalm.

"Against Thee, Thee only have I sinned. . . ." Yesterday afternoon, with no class to give (the last week before exams was reading period), she had been lying on her bed reading a mystery. She couldn't concentrate and thought first that her restlessness came from ignoring work she should be doing. She checked over the term papers, but all had been read and marked. She went to the typewriter and tried forming an intelligible sentence about Dr. Young and his *Night Thoughts*. "The vogue of melancholy . . ." but there illumination ended. Perhaps, she told herself, she was hungry;

[1] Jones, *op. cit*. P. 24. The Mohocks boasted of their crimes, calling them "sins of the gentleman," and were shocked to hear of a lowly criminal committing similar ones.

120

but in the kitchen vague nausea engulfed her. Sexual frustration, she rationalized, that must be the cause. She did what she could to relieve it, lying face down and pinching herself quickly to orgasm, but the restlessness remained. And then, two hours later, she was forced to admit the improbable, untenable cause: she wanted to go to church. So, changing from slacks to a skirt, placing a scarf over her head, she left for the nearest Catholic church. Inside, she walked past the holy-water font not daring to immerse her fingers. Up the aisle where hundreds of eyes leered at her from all corners (though the church was entirely unattended except for an old woman in black praying near the altar). She felt the sick shock of suddenly sensing an audience when one is alone in a room examining oneself naked in front of a full-length mirror and then feels eyes, and only after panic notices the cat. She seated herself in a pew, aware of nothing but heat and discomfort. She couldn't think, much less pray; she didn't know why she was here, was too ashamed of herself to move and thereby acknowledge her existence; she wanted only to be out but also wanted to cross herself. Her lucidity was torment, as though forced to watch a movie of herself going mad. A rational agnostic who had never genuflected, who throughout her life had been able to rely on her mind despite outward appearances, was now observing a second self, whom everyone would take for the real one, sitting in a pew of a church as garish and vulgar as a Woolworth's Christmas display. No interest in art or music could justify a millimeter of the scene. Her eighteenth-century sensibility was outraged; even if piety existed, to see it endure despite bad taste was unbearable. Never had she so hated herself. Hastily and surreptitiously, she made the sign of the cross and ran out. On the street, she whipped off her scarf, felt her heart clanging like an ambulance and knew there were tears on her face. She was ashamed, she hated herself, she went into a bar for three double whiskies and

121

later, when the sourness had gone, she thought that nothing she'd ever experienced was so painful as watching her mind betray her.

The psalm was over. His voice had lost its incantatory monotony and he was explaining: ". . . intimacy. Sin is the falling away from intimacy with God, and brings pain."

In other words, she thought, God is, like marriage, a serious affair. I'm mistress to a backward dog, marriage is made in heaven, but it's a *ménage à trois*.

After she'd gone, Father Niemans drank a glass of brandy and smoked a cigar. She was obviously in need of some orthodoxy, he reflected; the faith-hunger in her was stronger even than his appetite had been of late, and she wanted to devour what she couldn't digest, or be devoured by it. Strange, he thought, with all the glory she craved and from time to time seemed to feel, what she seemed to want was to fictionalize herself, to replace her dynamic nature with a static emblem. Dangerous, he realized. Comes close to John Scudley, who would rather be a thing than a man. She, too, was in the market for dreams and came to a priest because she thought him a good supplier. At what price, though? One thing was sure: her images of God were, as she said, emphatically (and promiscuously) anthropomorphic, a cross between Superman and Marlon Brando. She wanted to give herself to Him during a strenuous afternoon of shooting with 20,000 extras. Luckily, thought Father Niemans, whose stomach was being attacked by cramps of hunger, He endures despite His worshippers.

☞ 12

Next day was even worse. In the dream a stern, dog-eared priest forced her to bed with him. He fondled her; his lips, which should carry the word of God, now sucked her, and though he was repulsive she couldn't keep herself from responding ardently. She undressed and prepared to make the sacrifice but when she came to his room he was lying in the large feather bed with an extremely fat, ugly young man whose large red pimples and pale pustules were embedded everywhere in the fat of his face. She went down to the street unseen, where a group of nuns lined either side. The top nun, called Director or General (though she was only twenty-one, she had been a Dean of Students), shouted over to the novice in a red dress, "Now that basic training's over, how do you feel? Didn't I tell you it would be like the army?" Marya examined the nuns more closely and saw that all were wearing make-up; the novice was painted theatrically, with false eyelashes, pancake and iridescent shadow. Marya was sitting at a vanity applying cosmetics; she trickled some fluid on her forehead, making the sign of the cross and a voice was saying, "The juice of poperasts is thinnest and finest of all." She pressed her forehead against the mirror and heard a chorus (of nuns, probably; the voices were high) singing faintly:

> How many words make a teacher?
> How many drops make a sea?

> How many loves make a lover?
> How many lovers make me?
>
> Infallibility, infallibility,
> The only one for me.

And she spiraled out of the dream, sliding down coils, remembering the rings when she awoke. The poem was faint-
est, however, and by the time she had reached the typewriter she could remember only:

> How many loves make a lover?
> How many lovers make me?
>
> Infant ability, infant ability . . .

The rest was lost, but the energy left by dreams was so
strong that another line rose immediately:

> The bishoprics the Holy See,

and another after it, beginning a new poem of rhymed
couplets, which certainly didn't proceed from the dream
itself, but only from the giddy consciousness which the
dream left behind:

> I, a stranger and afraid,
> In a bed I never made.

That, she realized, would never do; it was only the waking
mind having a last romp of playfulness before admitting the
serious light of day.

She made herself coffee and the morning rolled towards
noon, a caboose uncoupled and moving down the tracks
alone, gathering speed. Brightness was falling from the air;
she was inhabited by images like a field of literature.
Phrases pricked her and, having forced an entrée, shot inside like sumptuous gate-crashers. "But as I rav'd and grew
more fierce and wild/ At every word,/ Me thought I heard
one calling, *Childe!*/ And I reply'd, *My Lord.*" Herbert, she

recognized.[1] They were so catholic in regard to century, those phrases, and fitted in so well with the company of lines assembled earlier that no one could know they hadn't been invited.

This had to stop; to be a voluptuary of English poetry beyond the age of twenty-one was unbecoming and rather absurd. She tried to concentrate on the phonemes in the lines, the grooved or slit fricatives, high back vowels, rounded or unrounded, consonants voiced or voiceless. But then another shot through: "To cease upon the midnight . . ." and she gave herself over to drowning in opulence.

Reviving a bit, she felt her mind turn slowly on its hinges, cast the backward glance and catch sight of deity. To go mad or become Catholic; both the same, a process leading to total capitulation. She admitted her main fear: simple conversion, however distasteful, could still be justified. After all, Swift was a mad Dean. But she was most afraid that the machinery of conversion wouldn't stop, that it would propel her along past Baptism and Communion until there'd be nothing left but to take the veil. Or become a saint. Infused by Him, pierced by Him . . . "Help," she said aloud and reached for the nearest book, a pamphlet of the Augustan Reprint Society.[2]

Reading John Gay was no help at all and she put him aside for the Lord's Prayer. There she was, she felt herself changing substance, the pores were growing into holes and then—thank God!—she was hungry and the image of a hamburger with relish crowded out all religion.

Next day she went to Mass. It was the twenty-first of May, the Sunday after Pentecost, four days before the Feast of Corpus Christi. Between the descent of the Holy Spirit, when babble was ended and men could speak in all tongues, and

[1] She was right. These are the last lines of "The Collar," by George Herbert (1593–1633).

[2] She was about to read: Gay, John, *The Present State of Wit* (*1711*). (Series One: *Essays on Wit*, No. 3.) The Augustan Reprint Society. Michigan, 1947.

the commemoration of the Eucharist, when the worshipper could partake of his Lord, Marya dressed herself in nacreous silk and went to hear Fr. Niemans say Mass. He entered wearing a green chasuble, whose rich fabric flowed like ancient gold over his alb.[1] He walked down the aisle with his sprinkler erect—the choir pitched high in praise—and watered the faithful with little jerks of his wrist. She felt the moisture from behind, a few drops ejaculated from the golden rod, and she trembled.

The service began; though she was uncomfortable—the bench was hard, the room too hot—she had regained her humor and now found a source of amusement in the hocus-pocus surrounding her. Women in hats and lace scarves sat stiff and intent in this mansion of love; a young girl over to the left held up her head as though it were made of the finest porcelain and could shatter in the twinkling of an eye. Her blond hair was erected in a strange edifice of stiff square curls glistening with silver sprinkles, ready for a later unveiling when the translucent headdress would be removed. Her apricot-colored lips drooped apart, her lashes trembled in the direction of the priest and her body was strained and tense, a watch wound too tight to move. Next to her, two little girls emptied the contents of their small plastic handbags and replaced them one by one. A five-year-old boy picked his nose and smeared the proceeds on the beige trousers of his dozing father.

". . . the Word gives life. A child is born and enters life with sound. He weeps to be born; we know he is alive when we hear the sound of his weeping. Crying is natural to man: his first sound after the silence of the womb. And why is this? Has not the Word come to all men? . . ." Heraclitus, thought Marya, and liked the way he spoke. That question

[1] *"Green,* the color of hope, is used on Sundays after the feasts of the Epiphany (Jan. 6) and Pentecost (movable), respectively."

"The *chasuble* . . . symbolizes charity and the yoke of the Lord."

"The *alb* . . . symbolizes freedom from sin."

1966 National Catholic Almanac. P. 272.

was difficult to answer, though. "Life it selfe is its owne vexation"—Henry Vaughan. "Why seems it so particular with thee, Hamlet?" Good God, she told herself, you can't confuse Catholicism with *everything*. ". . . yearning for the peace and love within the womb, where our mother nourished us with her own blood. Like the blood of Jesus Christ, it sustains us and transforms us from animals into men. As we grow older and until the day we die, we secretly yearn for that safety and love. We want to return to the Word at the beginning, erase the sounds of life, bypass language, ignore self-conscious speech and enter into the fulfillment of the Word. Which one of us has not found it difficult to express himself? Who hasn't tried to destroy the tower of Babel in his own mind? Who has ever found the right words for love?

"We know that words are our enemies. We attempt to flee them, but can never escape. . . ." He was marvelous; she wanted to take in every word but the tall young body under the alb and cincture was so straight that her eyes traveled along the folds of his robe, trying to penetrate, and her ears were too warm to unravel his discourse. The folds could be drawn apart, the curtain opened and the drama begin until the final decree: *Les jeux sont faits*. Opening the curtains on the nativity, the fulfillment of the fortunate fall, man redeemed again after Eve's rashness, peace after nakedness. ". . . and with the Word we find again the peace when we were unborn. It is not in death itself that we find peace. The grave is only a resting place and its peace is the joy preceding birth into new life. . . ." She realized suddenly that he was not speaking in metaphors and wanted to laugh. I believe . . . in the resurrection of the body and eternal cornflakes for breakfast and Elsie mooing in Elysian fields to be milked by Gabriel (God forbid that heaven be automated), so that her nourishing gift, unpasteurized (to which eternal life do germs go when they die?) may be poured on the golden flakes without ever (ah, heaven)

127

turning them soggy. Or do they have a different cereal? Instant Ichor, perhaps, or Ambrosia Krispies? Thank God, He's All-American. Music rose from the rear, organ and chorus. The congregation stood and joined in chanting.

The celebration of the Eucharist. He was straight and powerful, his face ruddy above the green. He bent, mouth opening, eyes closed, a close-up of his lips: moist, parted, meeting the Book in a kiss. A sound through the congregation like thighs smacking: she thought of the flabby, humid female flesh shuddering from benediction at the mouth. He stood tall again, the Host high over his head, light streaming in from behind and the white[1] satin lining of the chasuble shimmering around him: a periscope emerging from the sea. She felt dizzy and bright sparks exploded behind her lids. His arms stretched out for the blessing and she felt her body being screwed tightly, straining against the belt, the garter underneath, the elastic of her bra. At the altar, everything was in motion now, the bread and wine transubstantiated in the body of the priest to a fleshy spear pulsing with blood. Her hand moved down; the mouth, she thought, always the mouth, therefore, the lips. Heat became intolerable, she swayed on the bench, forced her hand up to clasp the other in prayer, a scream played in her throat but she crammed it down and then the chanting of Our Father began. It was over; she trembled slightly and thought, Thank God for ritual.

After the service, she had a cigarette first and then went to visit him in the apse. A piece of white linen lay across his shoulders, edged with eyelet around the neck. "What's that?" she asked, her fingers moving to touch it.

"This?" He retreated. "It's called an amice, to soak up the sweat." She smiled, thinking: And in the lamplight,

---

[1] "*White* is symbolic of joy, purity and innocence; it is used on feasts of the Holy Trinity, Our Lord, the Blessed Virgin, the angels, confessors, holy women not martyrs, and on Sundays after Easter."
1966 National Catholic Almanac. P. 272.

downed with soft brown hair, and held his eyes until he returned the smile. They held that gaze a few seconds and she thought it a smile without humor, like the smile of a man and woman after their second term of love, in gratitude and with wonder that they were not yet eclipsed. "I'm glad you came," he said.

"I am too."

"God love you."

She reached out for him, taking his arm to guide it to her breast, but he wrenched free, and after the first shock, his face put on an expression of sadness. "You don't want to do that, Marya. Marya. Listen to me." He spoke as though to a little girl. "You're too avaricious, you can't devour everything. Be still, let God love you."

"I wish He would," she said, her eyes still teasing him.

"No, not in your way. He won't come in the evening and pay for an hour's bout of love. You misinterpret the meaning of Omnipotent."

"How much," she asked, suddenly afraid, "do you know?"

"I didn't know much at first. I thought your interest in Catholicism showed a desire to find belief, or perhaps to examine the beliefs you already held. But Marya, you understand passion in one way only and think you're going to get extra payment for deviations. There's nothing I can do for you. You want to give up all responsibility, you want to be an object that's handed from one to the other. That's not the Christian way. We believe, you see, that man has dignity."

"And you think I have none."

"Marya . . . I'm sorry. There's nothing I can do for you. I can't be the pander between you and God."

"You . . . but . . . I was caught up in it. I could feel it, I had visions, my body was light."

"That word also means pregnant, as you know. You conceived your God in your own image in order to be destroyed

129

by him. One can lose oneself and find oneself again, but you just want to give yourself up. I'm sorry."

She was beginning to cry. She shook her head vigorously —he couldn't tell whether she was agreeing with him or trying to shake off his indictment—and ran out. He called out to her, "God bless you," and she ran faster, the tears flowing now. In the car, she had to wait a few minutes until she could focus. All she could think was, What the hell am I hanging around for? She lit another cigarette, told herself how pretty she looked, that though she might be superficial, nevertheless a lot of people seemed to like her, and eventually she could see clearly enough to drive home.

There, the better to justify her self-disgust, she ate everything she could find—stale crackers, hard cheese, chocolate syrup, an overripe banana—and the orgy lasted until she threw up. An hour later she went out to get the Sunday papers and there met Scudley, who told her he was starting work again tomorrow. She congratulated him perfunctorily and he suggested they celebrate the end of the school year with a trip to the country. She cocked her head, thought she might enjoy that, and told him to pick her up next Saturday around ten. "You have a cold, don't you?" she asked, because his voice was thick and nasal.

"Yeah," he said evasively. "Something I picked up at the supermarket."

"Hope you get better." She flapped her hand at him and left.

He watched her go and thought to himself that a cold in the head was, after all, better than being stone dead.

13

At least he could have the assurance that he'd been right all along. Molly was simply no good, a tramp. The day after she'd come to the store with a lot of fancy baloney about independence and the times being different now, something blowing in the wind, he'd seen her walking down the street with a little nigger no higher than his belly button. There she was, for all the world to see, walking down the street like she was the Queen of Sheba. That girl had bad blood, it was a good thing she wasn't living at home, he'd skin her like— he couldn't be responsible for what he'd do. And where did all that bad blood come from? Not through ten generations of MacGrogans, that was for sure, with all the women being virgins. He'd thought Isla's family could match up with anybody's as far as decency went, but somewhere there must have been a slip. He'd have to ask her about that, though it was a ticklish thing to do. She'd probably get offended. Well, in that case he'd be forced to tell her about their daughter and all the little niggers she was playing around with.

He leaned against the cash register and observed Scudley walk in. He was reminded of the young priest, that free-thinker. It was all very well for a priest to be tolerant; he didn't have any daughters. And of course Molly was wrong when she'd told her father he didn't know that something was blowing in the wind. He knew, all right. He felt it, smelled it, saw it on television and in the newspapers. But he wasn't going to stand around and let anybody break wind in his face. There was such a thing as decency, and decency was white. There was a place for those others—slightly below the Jews and above the Chinese—but that place wasn't abreast of Molly.

MacGrogan's views on life were simplistic, his sentimentality could be evoked as easily as could his spite and he had once given a Negro family the money necessary to send their son to college. If asked at any other time but this, he would be for integration, housing, the motto "one man, one vote" and would denounce the South as backward and narrow-minded. He was for Democracy, America, Free Enterprise and God. Negroes were necessary in the scheme of things; but Negroes (though he would never formulate it) were simply not people. They had their place, along with dogs, caterpillars and Orientals, and to see his daughter with one of them was comparable to seeing her fornicating with a goat.

"Hello, Mr. MacGrogan," said Scudley.

"What? Oh, it's you."

"Yes, sir."

"You look green around the gills. Are you sick or something?" he asked suspiciously.

"Oh no, it's nothing. Just something I picked up hanging around."

"Isn't it catching?"

"No, sir, just a hang-up."

"Well"—he was still dubious—"O.K. then."

"Thank you, sir." MacGrogan wondered for a moment if the guy wasn't trying to make fun of him—but no, he was too dumb. One of those who could never get away with anything.

Despite his cold, Scudley was pleased. He liked talking to the man under whose wife he had lain and whose rosebud feet he had seen in more detail, probably, than ever had her husband. Scudley felt almost avuncular towards MacGrogan; he knew how the guy's wife looked in the morning

132

and he knew Molly better than her father ever would, inside and out. They were one big happy family; here he was living, on and with the MacGrogans, and here he had tried to die. He should have known better. Who ever heard of someone dying in a supermarket? As unthinkable as having the canned julienne carrots go bad or the frozen meat patties become rancid. Nothing and no one changed form here. Still, it would have been nice; a kind of poetry about it, frozen to death between two sides of U.S. Prime. Scudley became philosophical: he had decided years before that everyone is born to a certain kind of death and that in dying, as in being born, there is no such thing as an accident. You started dying right from the beginning, and if you wanted to live right what you had to do was practice death often, until you had it down pat. Now he added to his philosophy the insight that all this dying was the only thing worth living for.

He was back again where he belonged and everything seemed, felt, smelled and looked the same. But Scudley had changed—nothing you could notice (except for his red eyes and generally swollen face) but he knew, walking past the meat, that something had vanished like a dream. His old life, the quiet superlife he had predictably led, no longer existed. For the past twelve days, he'd been like clothes in a washer, swirled around by a force which he couldn't control, and now he emerged spotless, like new, but with the memory of violence. He'd been released to a flood, his fantasies had become pornographic, he'd been involved in crime, drugs, had taken a mistress, felt hatred for a priest and had fallen in love. No more dreaming in the back room; no longer could he drift gently on currents of the day. He was receptive, now, to everything around him—or at least vulnerable—and so whatever he saw threatened him. On his rounds of deliveries he met people and they were not any more the same as a box of Brillo or a jar of mayonnaise. Now, he noticed whether a woman was attractive or not, how she moved, the tiredness around her mouth and the life of her hands. He saw the unhappiness of children, weariness on the faces of teen-agers, fear in old eyes. When he walked into a kitchen he could smell the food being prepared for dinner, saw stains and dirty dishes, observed the pile of laundry, heard sounds from the radio. Each delivery became as eventful as a circus: the wallpaper, plaster in need of repair, magazines and newspapers lying around (which articles had they been reading and where had they stopped?), hair that needed washing, a toilet running continually, stale crumbs, the odor of spoiled garbage, even—once—a trace of tears on the cheeks of a young housewife. Each delivery exhausted him. Responding to everything meant he was torn open in every house and with every person he met. Tableaux of pain were fixed in his mind; little gestures of hopelessness wouldn't remove themselves; news of the war coming over the radio presented him with torn bodies, gouged eyes, bloody children, mud, tears, high-pitched wailing, desperate girls in sleek, flimsy dresses, a dead eighteen-year-old with a bullet through his neck. Scudley couldn't stand it; by noon he felt he was going crazy. He found MacGrogan and begged to be allowed back to his old job. In a whim of generosity (and because one of the boys had walked out this morning), MacGrogan assented. Scudley almost kissed him; MacGrogan was the kindest man in the world and had never been properly appreciated.

But the change didn't help. Scudley couldn't avoid reading the faces of his co-workers and when they sang their usual songs he heard in the singing a kind of lament. The ladies who walked through the aisles with their shopping carts, hair in curlers or glistening with spray net, were just like those he delivered to. Even the objects roused Scudley's concern: a box of tissues fell, he retrieved it and almost wept to see the corner crushed. Pictures of kittens on cans of cat food made him smile; gurgling babies on pablum and disposable diapers opened his heart to love.

In the afternoon he saw Marya near the condiments and rushed to her. She greeted him affectionately with a firm handshake while her eyes caressed his face. "How good to see you back here! Congratulations."

He wanted to cry or bury himself in her. "Mare . . . Mare . . . I . . ."

"What is it, baby?"

"Somethings's happened. I . . . it's all too much."

"What is? The store?"

"Everything. People on the street, rosebud slippers, bags under the eyes . . ."

"Are you in love?"

"Mare! You . . . oh, but all of it."

He was called back. She waved him good-bye with "See you Saturday" and thought he probably had a fever, poor boy, the cold had developed into some kind of flu, he should be in bed and not working though it didn't make much difference with flus these days whether one attended to them or not. Probably a forty-eight-hour thing; it would pass.

But for the rest of the week Scudley suffered through his agony. Every moment brought new lacerations; he was so tender with Molly that she cried and asked him to bugger her; shoppers offered him enormous tips, but he refused all of them. After the first day his expansive, debilitating sympathy alternated with quick shoots of hate. He wanted to plant a bomb in the store, wanted to find a gun and shoot down all the shoppers, wanted to strangle them one after another. He would stick a butcher's knife between Mare's breasts and make love to her while stabbing (turkeys were once popular for their death spasms). He would rape a five-year-old child from behind, strangle a goat while violating it, organize an orgy with whips, boots, goats, men, women, nooses, clubs . . . but the fits would pass quickly, and with Molly he remained so gentle that she sobbed and begged him to hurt her.

His new emotions had nothing to do with the flu. His

135

dreams had been tampered with, he was exposed, his super-life had melted into the day-by-day life of an ordinary man, he couldn't help getting involved with the things around him and his emotions, untrained and unpolished, were those of a young child invaded by them for the first time. His hate, when he felt it, was of the intensity required to shoot Negroes in the back, but usually he felt love and that was almost too painful to bear.

He wanted Saturday to come quickly, so he could sit with Mare and tell her all of it. Her sharp mind would slice through this ooze that tormented him; she'd lead him from his feelings back to his senses again, she'd play with him like a toy and he could be a thing again, with no worries and nothing to do but put his head in her lap and smell the odor between her thighs. Saturday was the goal, if he survived. But Saturday kept stretching further away from him and meanwhile he was being used, not by Marya, but by some kind of power that allowed him no will of his own. He was being directed from outside, as helpless as he'd ever been, though in his helplessness he'd been given authority both to bless and kill.

Molly noticed a change in Scudley but had no idea of its depth or direction. She thought he was falling in love with her and responded by becoming hopelessly in love with him. While he was away at work she cleaned the apartment, did his laundry, sewed on buttons, went shopping and studied cookbooks. She had a drink prepared for him when he returned home in the evening and surprised him with an elaborate dinner every night. Though her surprises were more often shocks, she was too much in love to notice and he, seeing how concerned she was to please him, declared every dish the best he had ever tasted and manfully brought down a second helping of everything. They watched television in each other's arms and during the day Molly was too busy around the house to see any of her friends. When

Scudley kissed her, tiny pink flowers blossomed in a crystal ball behind her eyelids and sometimes the balls rolled down an alley padded with pink satin until they exploded in fireworks of green and gold. She had never been so happy; her body was hard and soft at the same time (hard on the outside, but fragile, like the most delicate stem of a crystal goblet; inside, she was soft as a warm spring) and though she couldn't sleep for happiness, she was never tired and felt so radiant she wondered how people could look at her without going blind. Translucent wings fluttered around her; moonstone was shining on her; she bent to stroke filthy cats and smiled happily at road workers who whistled at her. Mary Herself had never known such joy; it was hard as a formica shell and malleable as Silly Putty.

Bix told her it was impossible (the one time he saw her, on a Wednesday afternoon): she couldn't fall in love with someone who worked in a supermarket—didn't she remember how she felt about Jack? Going around to everyone squealing about her love like a little stuck pig? "That was different," she told him.

"Oh yeah? Don't get me wrong, chick, your Johnny's O.K., but a chick like you—you and he don't have anything in common."

"Yes we do," she said seriously. "Each other."

"Hey, baby—that sounds like you got it bad. You're different now. You look very happy, a little stoned. Anyway, it's cheaper'n pot."

She laughed. "He's like a whole mountain of pot—the Himalayas of pot."

Bix kissed her forehead and told his friends later that Molly would be out of circulation for a week or so.

And she was sure she had entered some kind of eternity, or at least the kindergarten of Eden. She sang old songs— "I can't believe that you're in love with me," "You're my baby now," "I want you, I need you, I love you"—and often paradise hugged her so tightly that she couldn't speak,

137

and only whimpered her exhilaration. Only, she wished Johnny would hurt her more so that when he was away she could still feel him through her own body. Somehow, though, during the times when they were actually making love, her heart was so full of pink crepe paper (the kind you can stretch) that she couldn't tell him to change the position.

All week her love expanded and swelled; by Friday, tiredness caught up with her and she was angry at him for not being worthy of the love he inspired. When she told him, "You should love me more," he stroked her hair sadly and comforted her. Furious, she bit him. He understood why she did this and kissed her eyes. His understanding made her violent. Her skin was flushed, fire licked at her eyes until the soft gray smoldered and became charcoal. "Lick my ass," she said. His hand was still patting her but she meant it and he obeyed.

Marya's week was filled with technicalities and last-minute business. Faculty meetings, exams, outlining of courses for next term, problems of grading (Could she, in conscience, give a draft-eligible young man a mark lower than B? But how unfair to the others, girls who might be applying to the same graduate school, married students who had done good work, Buff Willis and his future in steel, the two A students who, to be just, should stand out far above the others), and by Thursday she was too tired to find relief in the thought that this was her last exam and vacation was near. After the exam, students came up for a last-minute chat and she almost regretted that summer had come. Her little brood sustained her. She had fretted over them all year, been annoyed by them, vowed to stop teaching, proclaimed them all (in her mind) superlative idiots, but here they came, young faces charting their fear or pride of the exam, all of them grateful, trusting, happy to be free and yet already nostalgic about the years they would have left behind. Buff Willis waited until she was alone, told her (how dare he!)

138

that the exam had been very imaginative and asked if the date was on for tomorrow. Two girls, hair filthy, Bermudas spotless, were approaching with their bluebooks and hopefulness. She said "Yes" quickly; he shook her hand as the girls came up, said "Thanks, Dr. Poum, it's been great" and added, "Seven—a magic number in most societies. Seven exactly. *Cherchez la femme.*" She nodded in bewilderment that he should be so well trained in discretion. From how many illicit affairs had that boy received tuition?

Both girls were breathless (chain-smoking during the exam, thought Marya). She couldn't tell one from the other and their voices were indistinguishable. They told her: "It's been so great, Dr. Poum; this is the best class I had. You're the best teacher in the whole place—yes, you are; we all look forward to your class most."

"It was good to have you. What will you be doing now?"

Patiently, she listened to them and then to a series of other young men and women, telling of graduate school, technical schools, marriage, Peace Corps, advertising, Europe, summers in the mountains or by the sea, one girl would be an actress, three students were working on novels (no, she wouldn't mind if they sent them to her for comment), someone had an offer from Chase Manhattan, another from Bankers Trust; and she listened to the stream of opportunities, the beginnings of careers and lives, the onset of Reality (they all glowed, talking about what they would be doing), the forty different variations on the theme of Future, forty putative lives held out to her on platters in the hope that she would find them palatable. She nibbled a bit on each, for politeness' sake, and felt near crying. All her chickens, who would be voting for the first time this year or next, were about to be hatched and she realized she had grown fond of the eggs she sat on. How many would be crushed? How many in the next year or two? Commencement was a good word, but Conclusion might be more apt. She was experiencing a mild form of postnatal depression; the child ejected from the womb, the mother now felt tired and wondered if the entrance had been worth it. For all of them, life stretched out like an infinite rubber band; none of them was afraid now, just before graduation, that the band would snap in five years or ten and the solid slingshot holding them would be blasted apart with everything else. They were all rising, hatching, ascending into a blue freedom which was theirs by right to inherit two weeks from today when the hand moved the tassel from right to left and only in the eyes of a few was the vague fear that this rise into the blue might lead to explosion. Peace be with them, she thought, and almost wished for the grace to say, God bless them.

Then she surprised herself by opening wide her arms and embracing the girl on her left. She kissed the girl on both cheeks and moved back in embarrassment. She felt tears on her face and then the small group that remained all burst into tears, everyone came to be kissed or hugged and Marya embraced them all until they finally dispersed, each of them, including the professor, sniffling as he reluctantly walked away. Dr. Tapend saw Marya coming out of the building and was about to greet her, but she was too miserable and forlorn even to notice him.

Next day at seven, Buff Willis arrived in an English-tailored suit, beige gabardine with a flap at the back. He complimented her on her dress (black silk) and her earrings (topaz) and said they'd have dinner after the show, but why didn't they have a sandwich or something now? She said she had some things in the house—smoked oysters, a can of sprats, some olives—and they could eat that with their drinks. He nodded; his shoulders, under the well-built jacket, were held high and back and his body below moved with confidence. His self-assurance slightly terrified Marya; she understood situations easily and here was a very young man and an older woman, his teacher, but the personality

140

interfered with the role. She talked about the play they were going to see, about Albee as playwright (*"The Zoo Story* was his most successful piece; I'm afraid *Virginia Woolf* is ultimately unsatisfying because he attempts to make a statement and then doesn't present it in a believable manner. Did you notice the play follows closely the plot of *Mrs. Dalloway?"*), attempting to bring her intelligence to the aid of an undefined situation. She succeeded; he hadn't read the play or seen the movie and was forced to simply listen (as in class) while she expostulated. His silence, she saw, unsettled him, and when he leaned forward for his drink, he found he had too many limbs or that they were attached in the wrong places. His voice accommodated itself to the obtrusiveness of his body and Marya was relieved that his self-consciousness had been established, thereby restoring her sovereignty. By the time they left, he had drunk too much and was annoyed at himself for talking too little. She lightly took his arm and he turned to her, intending a look of deep significance, but—to her delight—he blushed instead. She held him tighter and smiled.

At intermission their conversation was formal; by the end of the play his poise had been restored and at the restaurant he was manly enough to reject the table offered them and insist on one in the corner meant for four. The meal was excellent; he suggested roast beef for her and from the skimpy wine list selected the only possible offering, a dry Chianti, emphasizing immediately (without asking her) that they wanted a full bottle, not half. Afterwards, he asked which she would prefer, brandy or a liqueur. She chose B & B but for the next drink joined him with brandy.

After dinner they returned by taxi and to her tentative "I don't suppose you'd like some more to drink . . . ?" he said if she didn't mind, he'd love to come up.

When he touched her hand, she almost dropped the glass. He removed it carefully, set it down and ran his hand up her shoulder, up over her neck, brought her face down to his and kissed her. She moved back and sat opposite him. They smiled at each other and she could feel the dangerous journey of her smile, moving in from her face, soon to illuminate and heat her body. A week ago today—the cop; then Scudley. Father Niemans—no. Even the approach to those thoughts brought blackness and she dispersed them with artificial light from her enforced smile. The light soon became more natural and she thought happily: Women are fickle, men are kind. It was so easy to feel the exhilaration, to be a little in love, to surrender to the quivering expectancy. She could fall in love with anyone who pleased her, and many could please her if she felt like falling in love. It was easy; it was pleasant; it was like rain in the tropics that came shuddering down and then disappeared quickly, leaving behind no memory but only brightness. She looked at his controlled smile; for him this incident would have its place and would not be allowed to interfere with emotions. It would be the epilogue to a splendid evening, the savory whose value was known only to connoisseurs. He would keep his heart out of it just as she kept away her mind. He blew her a kiss; her eyes registered the tenderness which had suddenly sprung up to accompany the thought that men fall in love more deeply than women do, but with much greater difficulty. It would be so hard for him to taste the full flavor of their interlude; for that to happen, you had to let sex breathe for a while in an atmosphere of love. The cop hadn't felt even the epicurean delight; Scudley was in love—poor boy—and this one would miss none of the spice but almost all of the sweetness. The taste would be pleasurable, but he wouldn't surrender to it. Only she would live completely on the joy of the ripe moment. They drank more and talked quixotically about events and people they had met along the way. Their eyes drank, quaffing lightly at first, then deeper draughts but without queasiness. They still talked, recounting little adventures as they traveled together on a quest neither of them acknowledged. Both

142

were free; they wandered easily among memories until, through talk or brandy, they drew so close to the perennially waiting sadness that they thought they understood each other. They compared songs they had sung as children and books they had read; and each of them, talking about himself as a child, was describing someone he had loved very much but had never known very well and who had died a long time ago. Two in the morning; neither imagined he was tired; the brandy was going down as steadily as oil in a lamp, stimulating them. They were very open with each other; discretion had disappeared along with a sense of separateness and each felt himself alone in a room with somebody in it. The direct influence of brandy had ceased a long time before, but nicotine worked through the head and sought release. "Let's go to bed," said Buff.

She nodded, stood up and guided him to the bedroom. They began undressing in silence; Marya looked out the window, saw a few stars and began to laugh. He looked at her in perplexity a moment; then they embraced, they kissed and he joined in the laughter. In bed, she felt pride in the way they took each other: two potentates bearing the solemn gift of themselves, offering one and accepting the other with pomp. They were both silent during the ceremony—quite brief, though elegant—of regal hospitality, and afterwards lay with their arms around each other, smiling. Their fingers explored each other's faces and Marya began, "In such a night"—the fingers fell away—"Stood Dido with a willow in her hand/ Upon the wild sea banks . . ."

"Dido?"

"Merchant of Venice, Act V, Scene 1, around line 10."

He laughed and embraced her. She went out to get their brandy glasses and he had a cigarette prepared for her when she returned. Her body was cool now and she rubbed against him for warmth. She remembered Scudley was coming at ten—about seven hours from now—and laughter rose in her like the smell of freshly baked bread. She was beautiful; all

143

things were full and mysterious and simple. Life and death were the same. Nothing more was needed; the crust of fresh bread crunched with a sound of happiness. They would meet again Sunday, and energy leaped through her as though day were just beginning after a night of deep sleep. She was young as her most frivolous thought; she was powerful because free and this freedom came from accepting necessity. Birds built nests, flowers ripened at their appointed time, the tides moved according to the moon; all things assumed their nature. They made love.

He was trying to get up and she put out an arm to stop him. "Wait," she whispered, "a few more minutes. Don't go just yet."

He brushed her off, sat up and sprang over her. He went to the bathroom; she turned on the light and heard him flush. She was alone here and called his name. When he didn't answer, she called again. At first she had called him caressingly; when he didn't answer, her voice became more and more urgent. He returned—still without speaking—and began to dress.

"Buff! What's the matter? Look at me! Look at me, Buff, for Christ's sake look at me."

He turned to her a face with no expression except smug blandness. She continued pleading, "What's the matter? Tell me, for Christ's sake. What's wrong? Come here. Sit down here. Here, sit down beside me on the bed. Buff!"

He resumed dressing, putting on each article of clothing with resoluteness and silence. She ran over, forced his hand to drop the sock it held and pressed tightly against him. He pushed her away. She stood, a few inches from him, trying to ask again but realizing, with a feeling like hysteria, that her voice wouldn't be steady and the tears would show through it. Finally he spoke, but he wouldn't look at her. "What the hell do you want from me now? I gave you what you were dying to have, didn't I? I satisfied you, didn't I?

You came. You must've come about three times. Isn't that enough?"

"Buff!" Her voice betrayed her. She wanted to tell him she hadn't come at all. She wanted to remind him that he had seemed to enjoy it. But she could only squawk and wait helplessly for his next words and his hatred.

"You're insatiable. You disgust me. You're just dying for it, aren't you? Dying to be screwed. Aren't you ashamed of yourself, a woman of your age? You're like an old whore, you just want to stuff that cunt of yours. And you're too fat. All that flesh sprawling over the bed, sweating like mad and dying to get laid. Well, I laid you, didn't I? I did what you told me, teacher." He was dressed now and, still without looking at her, walked out of the room. She saw he was white and shaking and told herself that his fury came from fear. He was very young; this act he had just committed must appear to him as incest. But she couldn't listen; she was terrified. She heard the door slam and threw herself blindly on the bed, then finished off the brandy in both glasses. She closed her eyes; her heart was pounding like a heavy hammer beating on a gong. Twentieth Century pictures. Ask not for whom the gong tolls. Night was suffocating her; she couldn't breathe and her eyelids wouldn't remain over her eyes. No thoughts could be admitted. She got out of bed, almost fell over, steadied herself and made her way to the bathroom. There she found what she wanted, took a handful of them, made a cup of her hands and slurped water into her mouth. Not all the pills would go down; she drank again until she forced them through her gullet. Then she returned to bed. Her eyes still twitched; night was everywhere around her, without end or amnesty. She tasted panic and it was stale and nauseating as nicotine. The twitching began to subside. The only cure was going through the night. She laid her hands by her sides and irrevocably entered.

145

☠☠ 14

They were curled into each other, though making love in the morning didn't come naturally to Scudley at all. It was nine-fifteen. He tried to push her away gently but she wouldn't let go. He tried to remove her arms from around his neck but she clung to him. "Johnny, don't go"—and she rubbed against him—"don't go, Johnny. Stay here with me."

"Can't." He tried to keep his voice low and loving but was impatient. Half an hour to shave, shower and dress before leaving for Mare's. "Let go now."

She wouldn't. She kissed his face, hairline, eyes and emitted little grunts; she kissed him full on the lips, worked her tongue between his teeth, groaned and moved her hand down. He pushed it away roughly; she said she loved him. "Please let me. Oh Johnny, I love you so much."

He'd been gentle at first but she stuck and dripped on him like honey. He tried to scrape her off, he reasoned with her, he pushed her more forcefully, but she came back. It was twenty-five after nine and he was becoming desperate. She oozed over him like a rapacious jellyfish, she would suffocate him. He kicked her, accidentally, and apologized. Her eyes became moist with love and drooped; her lips parted, she murmured, "Hurt me, baby, go ahead, I want you to hurt me." He looked at her, limp, half-dead, a fish gasping for air, its scaly body heaving on sand. He was terrified by her, disgusted; he hated her. There was no life in the eyes,

146

no blood in the body, no skin except scales; the creature's color was greenish-white; the fantasies came back—a dead witch-child buggered by a gorilla—he was held under water by a huge dead fish and it was sucking out the air, smothering him, drowning him in gills and scales, its clammy body holding him down, not letting him breathe. He had to get away; the eyes were marbles, the creature was preparing to suck his life out of him. His arms thrashed out, hit her; she moaned happily; he beat her, she urged him on—"Yes, Johnny, like that, more, hurt me more, I want to feel you in every bone, all over my skin, every muscle should ache from you, yes, yes, like that, more"—and his hands found her collarbone, the delicate bone of a fish, the bone you choke on, and pressed. His thumbs revolved in semicircle and his hands followed until they were encircling the neck. They pressed; her eyes burst open, lips parted as though to speak (green fish lips sucking the air, sucking oxygen out of the air), the eyes were two round balls of horror, dull marbles stuck in red-veined chalk, something rumbled in the neck, something was trying to force its way up and out, he pressed harder, held it down, squashed it, pushed it back, wrung the neck. The face didn't move any more, the eyes were wide open and unblinking, something cracked somewhere (biting out the brain of the octopus) and the tentacles loosened their hold; he was free again and let go. The head flopped back, the neck was ugly and purple. He'd killed the sea-monster; he turned to tell Molly, but Molly was hideous, green, purple and white, a monstrosity left on the beach to die.

He jumped out of bed, took a quick shower, didn't bother to shave, threw on his clothes and went back to look. The two gray marbles stared at him from a green face. He breathed on it and the monster's mask didn't twitch. He tried to call "Molly," but no sound came from him except little yelps he couldn't control. And then he closed his mouth

147

and didn't try to say anything any more. What difference did it make? Who cared? If he didn't hurry, he'd be late.

He rang the bell, knocked, kicked and waited ten minutes before he realized the door was unlocked. He entered, calling "Mare," but there was no answer. He was feverish; the flu was still fiercely in him; he called and, hallucinated, the sound of his voice exploded in bright purple flashes and suns burst blood. Dwarfs clung to the lighting fixtures and leered at him. In the bedroom, he saw her—his groin felt her first, with a sharp kick in the balls and then his kidneys started to melt. "M . . . Mm . . . Ma . . . Ma . . ." It wouldn't come out, stuck somewhere in the fur-lined gullet. This looked like Molly but its face was darker. Blue, green, purple—angry coloration streaked her face and the eyes wouldn't open. She was sleeping, said his mind, and the calcium of his bones melted, disintegrated, flaked away until his limbs were immovable. "She's sleeping," said his parietal lobes, but on either side the hemispheres echoed, "She's dead." He was somehow propelled to the bathroom, where he vomited over the floor, the bathmat, some vomit splashing to the shower curtain and the towels. He came back and looked at Mare. He felt no shock now, no sadness; he was purified and lighter than air. He wondered how they'd take their ride to the country. The car first. Her handbag was in the living room, lying on the floor beside the coffee table. He went through it, throwing out its contents until he found the car keys. He slipped these in his pocket, jumped up and down on the handbag until it was crushed and dead, and went out, making sure the door would remain unlocked.

After only five minutes, he found the car just around the corner and he sang aloud to it as he approached, "Oh say, can you see/ By the Triumph's blue light/ What so proudly we screamed/ At the twilight's last gleaming?" He entered, and while looking for the ignition, burped up little pockets of song: "rockets' red glare," "bombs bursting," "through the night," "land of the free." He started her up, crashed into the car parked behind, stalled, and started her up again. After about fifteen minutes, with the car trembling, wheezing, stalling and jerking, he was able to get her out of the hole. A few minutes more and he brought her in front of the service exit, where he alighted and pocketed the keys.

He went up in the service elevator and returned to Mare's apartment. She was still where he'd left her and he took the sheet she was lying on, wrapped her in it, rolled her over and over so the sheet would stay closed. He thought of kissing her before she was all packaged up, but there was no time for that now. He tried to pick her up and fell; he righted himself and tried again, pulling at the arms. Something snapped; she was extremely heavy. He rolled her down to the floor, fixed the sheet again and dragged her to the door. The sheet was getting dirty; that meant the floor hadn't been cleaned for a while. Something had to be done about that. He parked her behind the door, sweeping up her limbs into a compact bundle and looked out to see if anyone was coming. The hall was empty. He picked her up, forgetting that he hadn't the strength to do it, and carried her to the service elevator, where he again parked her while he rang. He noticed he had no breath any more; some sharp icicle-type thing was cutting through his lungs, but that was all right, you could always breathe, he'd been breathing all his life; the important thing now was taking a ride in the country with Mare at his side. The elevator came, he prodded her into it, pressed button B and sat on her until they arrived in the basement, where he picked her up, flung her over his shoulder like a knapsack, patted her buttocks, assured her it wouldn't be long, they'd be out in the fresh air soon, she should hold her breath a little while longer. He carried her down the ramp and out to the

149

street, where an elderly couple and two teen-age boys stared at him. The old lady turned questioningly to her husband but he shrugged his shoulders and pushed her along, almost knocking the cane out of her hand.

Scudley, collecting icicles in his diaphragm, locomoted to the car. One of the boys spat and called, "Hey, man, whatcha got there, a corpse?"

Scudley stood on his dignity and didn't answer. The boys followed him to the car, opened the door for him and watched him drop Marya on the seat. "Was that your wife?" asked the other boy. "Or your mother?" Scudley didn't deign to answer. He went around to the driver's seat, got in, found the keys in his pocket, exactly where he'd left them, and without hesitation started the motor. The boys lounged against the body until the explosive sound of back-firing scared them off. Since there was no car in front of him, Scudley couldn't crash into it. The boys watched his maneuvers with sardonic admiration and one told the other, "I never seen a lousier driver since I been born."

"Yeah," agreed his friend, "this cat takes the cake. You think he stole the car, too, after murdering his mother?"

"Could be. He's quite a cat."

"Yeah." Scudley heard no more and roared off. Those kids should be locked up, he thought, disturbing the peace. Scudley kept the car in second gear despite its protests and wheezed through town, taking no notice of the different colored lights and the large signs advising him to stop or turn or go in one direction only. Brakes screeched around him, names were hurled at him and Marya, but they were both deaf to insults. He drove on, through the elm-lined streets, the icicles slowly beginning to melt, his Mare at his side silent and acquiescent; and when he drove past the MacGrogans' house he gave a nod. When they passed the town limit, Scudley slowed down and unwrapped Marya with his right hand. She began to slip; he yanked her up again, admiring his one-armed prowess. It wasn't easy, he assured himself, to unwrap a woman with one hand and keep her level with you while driving a car. The whole business took almost ten minutes, but at the end he had her completely unwrapped with her head resting cozily on his shoulder. He pressed on the accelerator and his right arm was holding her. But the car protested and Scudley remembered about the other gears. Bringing back his arm, he used it to manipulate the shift, and moved first into third, then into fourth gear. They were on the highway now and doing sixty-five. His arm was around Marya again and her face pushed against his chest when he reached to turn on the radio. He settled back again and a song, vaguely familiar, blared at them:

> Let me tell you, babe,
> You must be dreamin',
> The world ain't spinnin'
> Just for you alone.

They drove happily, the two of them in the sky-blue convertible, tearing down the highway as the song faded for the commercial: a nasty little child uttered its first words and they were a whining plea to its mother to go out and get more sausages. Station break: weather ("Sixty-eight degrees, fair and sunny with a chance of showers tonight")—pity, that; he didn't want showers to interfere. A voice exploded from the bottom of a well or inkpot: "Does your sink gurgle? bubble? gasp for air?"

"Yeah," answered a flat, sprawling female voice, "But that's 'cause you're sitting on the drain. Whatcha doing in my sink anyway?"

"I'm Bob Eagle's boy, straight out of the red-white-and-blue can. I'm here to protect your drain. . . ."

"If my husband comes home and finds you here, he'd flush you down. Say, I didn't notice before—you're not much bigger than a lump of sugar, are you?"

151

"But I melt much more easily. Just sprinkle me . . ." A siren was screeching behind them; he pressed down and the needle moved to seventy. Another song, an old one, he could remember it from his childhood but with slower beat:

> Don't sit under the apple tree
> With anyone else but me   (oh baby),
> Anyone else but me   (oh baby),
> Anyone else but me. . . .

He couldn't hear it any more, the wind was too loud and the sirens had been turned up. He drove faster, 75, 80, 90 and the car took off on its own. It shook, it weaved back and forth, it seemed to jump in the air and Scudley had no control over it. Happily, he held Mare more closely and noticed how bright the sun was. They passed all other cars, sirens wailed and he liked the sound, it was predictable and he had become used to it in a very short time. He pressed Mare to him and she was lying over his right side. "Mare," he told her, "Mare, I love you, Mare. I love you so much it hurts, like a great enormous snowdrift pushing through me and all the icicles going bang bang bang. When I kiss you, baby, everything goes blue inside, it all melts down like the fucking sea and it's all blue, blue patterns, sky blue, pale blue; I drown in you, Mare baby, blue calico like we had at home and Wedgwood, little blue tongues licking at me like a pussy. There was this flag, see? She had one flying all the time and in the first grade I saluted like a soldier, not the way kids do now with a hand over the heart, no sir, I had it up there, saluting like a real soldier. Old Glory it is, Mare, and when you touch me it goes red, a bullfighter's cape, blood blood, the sun's all red and the wine drips down from it, yum, yum, they lance it. Yeah, baby, they lance that old pimple of a sun and whee! blood spurts out, great blobs of redred, like a heart you grab out of a chest, dripping into tall glasses. Why don't you talk to me, Mare? I'm lonely. She waves and waves and

152

flaps and cackles. They wrap you up in her when you die and you're glory-bound. Everything's shining red, see it? Ooo, look see the rain come down red, spurting blood sun and that great fucking slaughterhouse. That's where we been, you and me, in the great big slaughterhouse, you can freeze the blood and poof! like that it stops. Oh, mother! What a mother! Deep in there where the blood comes dripping red"—he was doing 108 now, as fast as the car would go—"and it's freezing into stripes, red and white, is the blood our fathers spilled, white again, you're all white, is the freedom they fulfilled blue says be true to me and to you—look at that! it's white, snowing, the stars are frozen, they said showers tonight, a drag, the sky's in the freezer, oh fuck the sun, baby, it's white!" He let go the wheel and took her in his arms.

"John Scudley again," said the attendant, "or what's left of him, the bastard."
"Dead, is he?"
"I'll say."
"Killed himself again?"
"An accident. Here, help me scrape up the mess."

Both bodies were so mashed that autopsy was useless. They were cremated and the ashes disseminated according to the laws of the state. At the service for Marya, Father Niemans took the liberty of saying a few words. He spoke haltingly and, as he had explained to the university officials in charge, was here more as a friend than as priest. Marya Poum had not been Catholic and he would not claim her soul for the Church. He spoke to a large assembly; so many faculty members and so many of her former students had shown up that most were forced to stand during the entire service. After summing up her virtues (whimpering and sniffing came from all sides), Father Niemans said,

153

". . . she loved God and her suffering was short. I can't ask you to pray for her; she would have wanted no prayers. Her life was passionate; her firmest belief was in humor. Her irreverence, like that of Dr. Samuel Johnson, whom she greatly admired, was a foil against her terror of God and night. She once quoted to me some words of a modern poet —'Avoid deep places and die blaspheming.' None of us can know what she was thinking when she died, but let us hope, and pray if we can, that her last thought was love. . . ." Here his voice broke, and though he had wanted to speak of the Supreme Power, he was powerless even to say "Amen." As he walked away, he heard a peculiar sound and saw that a tall young man at the back was laughing.

At Molly MacGrogan's funeral he was more eloquent and Catholic. Jo-jo cried when the Father spoke about the tragedy of death at such a young age, but Bix was tight with fury when he heard the phrases of everlasting life. Isla MacGrogan heard nothing but the beating of her heart and her husband was carrying on a private conversation with the saints.

At Scudley's rites, a municipal employee said a few words, the national anthem was played and the ashes flung to the winds, which carried them under spacious skies across the fruited plain; and deposited them at the base of a tree where a mother eagle in her nest flapped powerful wings and laid another egg.